Overhead Assets

by Nelson R. Gomm

© Copyright 2019 Nelson R. Gomm

ISBN 978-1-63393-864-9

Published by

◄ köehlerbooks ™

210 60th Street
Virginia Beach, VA 23451
800-435-4811
www.koehlerbooks.com

OVERHEAD ASSETS

NELSON R. GOMM

VIRGINIA BEACH
CAPE CHARLES

To my wife, Laurie, of forty-nine great years together

ACRONYMS

AFB	Air Force Base
AM	Amplitude Modulation
CIA	Central Intelligence Agency
CEO	Chief Executive Officer
CoB	Close of Business
DARPA	Defense Advanced Research Projects Agency
DEW	Directed Energy Weapon
DoD	Department of Defense (US)
DTED	Digital Terrain Elevation Data
ELINT	Electronic Intelligence
EMP	Electromagnetic Pulse
ENVG	Enhanced NVG
FAA	Federal Aviation Administration
FBI	Federal Bureau of Investigation
FM	Frequency Modulation
FSB	Federal Security Service of the Russian Federation (successor to the KGB)
GEO	Geosynchronous Earth Orbit (satellites)
EO	Electro-Optical (spectrum)
H&K	Heckler & Koch (gun manufacturers)
HPM	High-Powered Microwave
HQ	Headquarters
IR	Infrared (spectrum)
ITK	Ispravitelno-Trudovaya Koloniya (Russian Corrective Labor Colony)
LED	Light emitting diode
LEO	Low Earth Orbit (satellites)
MEO	Medium Earth Orbit (satellites)
MI6	Military Intelligence Section 6 (UK)
MOS	Military Occupational Specialty
MRAP	Mine-Resistant/Ambush Protected (vehicle)
MSL	Mean Sea Level (altitude)
NGA	National Geospatial-Intelligence Agency
NRO	National Reconnaissance Office

NSA	National Security Agency
NVG	Night Vision Goggles
ODA	Operational Detachment Alpha (Army Green Berets)
OTH	Over-the-Horizon
PM	Makarov Pistol (Russian)
POTUS	President of the United States
RIA	Russian Information Agency-Novosti (Russia's official news agency)
RoE	Rules of Engagement
RTB	Return-to-Base
SAM	Surface-to-Air Missile
SAR	Special Access Required
SATCOM	Satellite Communications
SBSS	Space-Based Surveillance System
SBT	Seal Boat Team
SCIF	Sensitive Compartmented Information Facility
SIGINT	Signals Intelligence
SIPRNet	Secret Internet Protocol Router Network
SI/TK	Special Intelligence/Talent Keyhole
SLR	Side-looking Radar
SME	Subject Matter Expert
SOCOM	Special Operations Command
SOF	Special Operations Force
STB	Science & Technology Branch (FBI)
STE	Secure Terminal Equipment (Encrypted telephone)
SWAT	Special Weapons and Tactics
TASS	Russian News Agency
TEL	Transporter/Erector/Launcher
UHF	Ultra High Frequency (radio)
USSTRATCOM	US Strategic Command
UTC	Universal Coordinated Time
VHF	Very High Frequency (radio)
WMD	Weapon of Mass Destruction
XO	Executive Officer

"What counts is not necessarily the size of the dog in the fight;

it's the size of the fight in the dog."

DWIGHT D. EISENHOWER

MAP OF BAIKONUR REGION

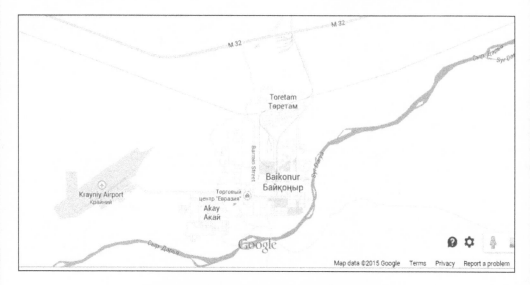

BAIKONUR AND AIRPORT

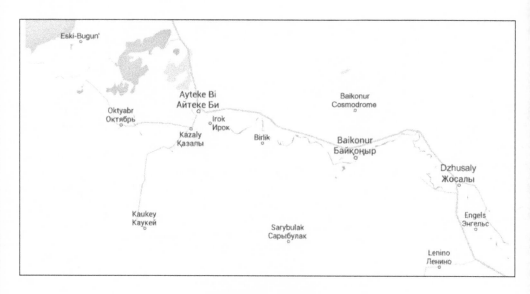

ALONG M32
KAZAKHSTAN

PREFACE

ON ANY DARK and clear night, you can see satellites whizzing by in low earth orbit (LEO). The biggest and brightest is the International Space Station (ISS). There are many commercial satellites in LEO launched by many nations to aid in communication, weather, navigation, and land survey. However, there are also satellites in orbit with the sole purpose of aiding the military with intelligence gathering systems that employ telescopes, signal intercept, spectrum analyzers, EMP and infrared sensors, and oceanic radars—or, as the military refers to them, "overhead assets." Future defense of these critical military satellite systems will depend on the development of satellite-based threat sensors and defensive weapons. Offensive "space" weapons of mass destruction (WMD), although banned by international treaty, will likely be developed and may already be in pre-deployment lab testing. The following fictional scenario could very well become reality.

1

Farmhouse near the Baikonur Cosmodrome, Kazakhstan

THE COVERT OPERATIONS team had just finished adjusting both super high frequency antennas in preparation for the intercepts. It was now very dark and, although their eyes had adapted, they used low-level red LED headlamps to perform the final calibrations and adjustments. Lieutenant Colonel Steve Walker, the team leader, had performed many night ops with the latest low-light and infrared AN/PSQ-20 enhanced night vision goggles, or ENVGs, which always provided a distinct advantage. However, they were not necessary inside the farmhouse.

Walker declared in his typical monotone, "We only have another ten minutes before the satellite comes into view. Let's not screw this one up, people!"

The "people" were a specialized team of technical operators and CIA operatives, handpicked from the best the United States Department of Defense had to offer. Most of them had worked together on similar field assignments, but this one was classified via presidential directive—TOP SECRET WEBMAZE. There were only a handful of people in the US government with that clearance, and access was briefed personally by Under Secretary of Defense Roy Sheffield.

In order to effectively execute these intercept missions with the smallest possible footprint, the team was limited to its leader, a datalink communications expert, a satellite expert, a local CIA operative, and two special forces operators trained in clandestine weapons, tactics, and defensive combat. This team was more specialized but similar to a typical Army Special Forces Operational Detachment Alpha team.

Susan "Mac" MacDonald, the team's satellite expert, called out, "Cosmos 2455 has just come up over the horizon! It should be within comm distance in another five minutes. Brian—get ready!"

As the satellite approached from the southwest, it was predicted to pass overhead at exactly 2328 local, almost midnight. Her highly classified ultrathin notebook computer had all known US and foreign satellite orbits programmed. She could also predict when surveillance satellites were coming into view.

The comm expert, Captain Brian Mathers, intently watched the signal strength build on the display as the satellite approached. Because it was whizzing along at over 17,000 mph, the Doppler shift was highest just above the horizon during initial acquisition. The classified signal acquisition and tracking software was developed by the RANOX Corporation at the Cambridge office in the weeks since the launch of Cosmos 2455 from the Baikonur Cosmodrome, Kazakhstan. The software and miniaturized radio were developed and tested within a week of the first signal intercepts reported by the DoD's overhead assets— Aquacade and Trumpet SIGINT satellites.

Just as the satellite was at near-full signal strength, the telemetry channel opened up at the Baikonur Cosmodrome. Brian announced, "Control signals have commenced! Recording activated!"

Walker got a call on his Iridium 9505A Type-1 encrypted satphone—and he did not look pleased. The team watched his reaction and waited for the news. Any incoming calls at this phase of a mission were never a good sign.

"Yes sir, understood." Walker ended the call and blurted, "Operations will cease—immediately! We've been ordered to stand down. NSA notified General Black that there's been a compromise of the mission. Break it down and pack it up!"

One of the two Ranger operatives, Sergeant Jared D. "JD" Stone, yelled, "Outer perimeter breached!"

Staff Sergeant Rick Guerrier, who just put on his NVGs, said, "Two vehicles comin' up the road; they're GAZ Tigers!"

The GAZ was the Russian Federation's equivalent of the DoD's High Mobility Multipurpose Wheeled Vehicle, or Humvee, and each could carry four heavily armed soldiers.

Walker commanded, "Break everything down and get to the tunnel. NOW!" They had less than ninety seconds to pack everything up and escape through the basement subfloor tunnel.

Everything and everyone were accounted for as Walker watched the two GAZ vehicles approach. He scanned the room for a last check and noticed Brian had left a backup battery under a table. He grabbed it and practically jumped into the tunnel in two bounds. With both Ford Fiestas parked on the other side of the field, there was no sign of them having been there.

The tunnel was unlit and barely big enough to crawl through—challenging enough without having to drag all their equipment with them. Local CIA operative Vladimir Ivanov had planned for this over eight years ago when the CIA required clandestine access to the Baikonur Cosmodrome. Vladimir bought the old farmhouse for a song in the late 1990s when the Russian government was cash poor. He used a phony business name as the landowner.

Vladimir, leading the way with his red headlight switched to low-light white, whispered in a strong Russian accent, "Come this way. Do not speak above a whisper." The tunnel led to a small storage shed about eighty meters away.

Susan and Brian struggled as their mission equipment bags periodically hit the tunnel floor. The two Rangers and Walker kept their Glock 19s and H&K MP-5SDs at the ready—the MP-5SDs were specially designed for full suppression firing a subsonic 9mm round. Vladimir assumed that Walker remembered the booby trap under the floor in case the tunnel was discovered.

Aboveground, the two GAZ vehicles unloaded eight men with AK-74M assault rifles, who immediately surrounded the farmhouse. The lead soldier was a captain, designated by the four small stars on his epaulette, and the detail was manned by sergeants with stripes similar to the US Army. The captain quietly approached the front door looking for any signs of activity and, finding none, checked the door for booby traps. He and two of his detail walked in and fanned out, searching every nook and cranny in the building. After each yelled out "clear" in Russian, the captain pulled out a small walkie-talkie device and reported.

"Sir, the farmhouse is empty—no signs of activity. Further instructions?"

The voice at the other end commanded in Russian, "That is not possible!! Search again and stay there through daybreak if necessary."

Not particularly convinced there was a serious threat, the captain and his men went inside and, after a few minutes, settled in for an early morning snooze. To the captain, these details were boring and not exactly career advancing assignments.

The team of six quietly exited the storage shed one by one as soon as Rick, still wearing the NVGs, confirmed that all the soldiers went into the farmhouse. They walked in single file to the edge of a poplar grove about 100 yards from the shed. Then they ran another sixty yards to the road, with the tree grove behind them. Last out was Rick.

The two Ford Fiestas were parked where they left them earlier. It was now almost midnight and silent. Since it was a new moon, it was also very dark except for the spillover light from the Baikonur Cosmodrome. It was warm this time of year but a bit chilly at night.

They split up three and three, jumped into the Fiestas, started the engines, and drove off. The Fiestas were extremely quiet—a well-built vehicle that easily dominated the Russian market. The small road south and west of the cosmodrome was unlit and in need of repair. With Vladimir directing from the lead Fiesta, they drove for an hour north on M32 to an abandoned farm machinery storage building. They quickly hid the Fiestas inside an old adjacent barn. This was another of Vladimir's projects. He was surprisingly thorough; for the kind of money the CIA was spending, he was expected to be. Vladimir bought the abandoned farmhouse at an auction with CIA funds and was recorded as the landowner.

They were exhausted. Susan grunted, "This place isn't too bad, just not quite like the Sputnik."

The Sputnik Hotel was not fancy but had all the amenities. With 120 rooms, it was one of the largest hotels in Baikonur. Unfortunately, the authorities would be watching for late-night vehicle activity, so they had to stay at the farmhouse until morning. Vladimir was instantly the hero when he opened a giant refrigerator behind a fake storage wall. It was stocked with eggs, bacon, butter, yogurt, cold cuts, water bottles, frozen vegetables, and fruit—enough to last the team a week. There was a makeshift mini stovetop in a side room that also had a pantry filled with pots, pans, bread, crackers, coffee, and canned food. Vladimir gave them a quick tour and said, focusing on Susan, "It's not the Sputnik, but we should be safe here for the night."

They all grabbed some food and then, much to the team's delight, Vladimir brought out some Baltika No. 3 beer, which was a slightly stronger version of Bass Ale. Since the fall of the Soviet empire, beer had become more coveted, but vodka was still king.

Susan was pleasantly surprised. "Vladimir, you outdid yourself! So, where are the beds and bathrooms?" Vladimir pointed to a door and said, in his strong Russian accent, "The bathroom is in there, but, sorry, no beds. We have cots and blankets in there for up to fifteen."

Walker said, "Mac's right. This place is awesome. Yeah, it's not like home, but it will do for now. Eat and get some sleep. After breakfast, I'll contact the Center and get further instructions."

Brian, usually passive, was elated at the food selection. "Hell, this fridge is stocked better than mine! If it's okay with you guys, I'll cook scrambled eggs and bacon for breakfast."

Rick quickly piped up. "Make mine crispy!" Jared followed with, "I like my bacon a little rubbery!" Brian yelled back, "You'll get it the way I cook it!"

Walker stepped in. "Rick, JD—check all the weapons and ammo. Make sure all the cell phones, the satphone, temblors and mission equipment batteries are charged. You guys decide the guard duty coverage."

Rick pulled out a ten-ruble coin and said to Jared, "Heads or tails?"

Jared asked, "Which side is heads, the ten or the double eagle?"

Rick said, "Let's call the ten side heads."

"Then I call tails—the double eagle!" said Jared.

Rick flipped the coin and slapped it on the back of his wrist. "Tails it is. Your call on who does the first shift."

"I'll do the first. I can't sleep now anyway. I'll get you at 0400," said Jared.

"Okay, I'll wake you for breakfast." After they checked the weapons and set up the chargers, the team set up the cots and got some sleep.

2

Two Weeks Earlier

PRESIDENT RYAN MARR was being briefed in the White House Situation Room on the latest Russian Federation rocket launch from Kazakhstan. Having been in office for only sixteen months, Marr was relatively new to major intelligence threat reports. CIA director Daniel Greenway and NSA director Anthony Duffy had called the meeting because of a parallel intelligence report coming out of the US Embassy in Astana, Kazakhstan.

After handing the intelligence briefing and a few separate reports to the president, Greenway gave his report.

"Sir, ten hours before the launch of Cosmos 2455, a woman by the name of Marzhan Kanat walked into the US Embassy in Astana Kazakhstan asking for asylum. She claims to be an engineer at the Baikonur Cosmodrome rocket launch facilities and reported that the Russian Federation will be launching a satellite that is rumored to be a weapon system."

Director Duffy added, "And according to experts from our laser tracking facility at Westford Mass and the analysis of the Space-Based Surveillance System infrared imaging and tracking satellite data, Cosmos 2455 is almost twice the size of their largest reconnaissance satellite."

President Marr was visibly concerned. "Should we believe what this woman claims? Did anyone check her out? I understand that some communications satellites are pretty large."

"Mr. President, sir, we did a thorough background check on her and she's legit," Greenway said. "She also gave us a detailed description of the satellite and some of its features. It's all in the CIA intelligence report."

Danny Greenway was no stranger to vetting people, having done this often while coming up through the ranks at the CIA.

Director Duffy, an expert on satellite optics, added, "Sir, the information we have on Cosmos 2455 is limited at this time, but we are researching every resource available to find more."

Anthony Duffy was a geeky engineer who gravitated to space optics after graduating the Rensselaer Polytechnic Institute with a master's in engineering science. He started designing space optics for the DoD and eventually wound up as CEO at Itek Optics.

Not satisfied with Duffy's report, President Marr probed. "So, is there anything we can do without stirring up a major international controversy? What have we done in the past? Do we know for certain whether or not this is a weaponized satellite?"

"Sir, I'd like to bring in my two experts on this," Greenway said, "USAF chief of staff General Erik Hollaway and the new head of Space Command, General Jamie Tillet."

"Yes—of course. Bring them in!"

After Hollaway and Tillet were seated, the president demanded, "What will it take to determine what Cosmos

2455 is all about? I do not want the Russians to know about our capabilities, but we have got to find out what they are up to!"

All this concern was heightened by the event of February 10, 2009, that saw Cosmos 2251 slam into Iridium 33, disrupting US satellite communications for days. Although NASA publicly claimed that the Russian satellite was not maneuverable, it was noted by some space tracker enthusiasts that Cosmos 2251 appeared to have moved slightly in its orbit just before impact.

General Tillet was concerned about the attendees at the meeting, some of whom he was not certain were cleared for access to WEBMAZE. He looked around the room for Under Secretary of Defense Sheffield, who was responsible for all TOP SECRET WEBMAZE clearances, but did not see him at the table.

"Mr. President, sir, I need assurance that everyone in this room is cleared for TOP SECRET WEBMAZE!" Tillet said. The codename *WEBMAZE* itself was top secret, and Tillet was always nervous when briefing on WEBMAZE. *What a big mess I'll have to clean up if not everyone in the room is cleared to that level*, he thought.

Secretary of Defense Lance Denzer sat up and bellowed, "We're all cleared for WEBMAZE. Start the briefing, General—now, please!"

It wasn't his place to question the defense secretary, so General Tillet proceeded with the top secret briefing. After the classified CD was inserted into the tower computer, Tillet started.

"Sir, a Soviet satellite, Cosmos 954, launched on September 18, 1977, was a Radar Ocean Reconnaissance Satellite capable of detecting US Navy submarine activity around the globe." A graphic depicting the USSR RORSAT was projected on the screen. "It was considered a threat to our nuclear submarine operations—the third leg of the nuclear triad. A special team of satellite telemetry signals experts were successful in intercepting the control signals of Cosmos 954 two months after launch." A graphic depicting the satellite and ground control telemetry signals appeared on the next screen—with the signal intercept radios shown in close proximity to the cosmodrome. "The operation was classified TOP SECRET WEBMAZE. There were two major components to the operation: signals intelligence and clandestine control."

"Although the satellite's radar data downlink was encrypted, the control signals were not. Sanctioned by then-president Jimmy Carter—a submariner by training—a special team was assembled to clandestinely control the satellite with the goal to prevent the Soviets from finding and tracking our nuclear submarine fleet. The US was clandestinely controlling Cosmos 954, pushing it off orbit, to force the Soviets to use up all the maneuvering thruster fuel attempting to keep it in reconnaissance orbits. The operation was successful, and the Soviets thought that the satellite was unstable. Unfortunately, Cosmos 954 was nuclear powered and eventually deorbited and crashed into Canada's Northwest Territories. Joint US/Canadian Operation 'Morning Light' was executed to find any remnants of the reactor fuel."

"So, General, let me get this straight," the president said. "The DoD took control of a Soviet nuclear-powered satellite and caused it to crash into Canada?"

The general was unapologetic. "Yes sir."

"And the WEBMAZE capability became a new DoD mission, right?" the president asked.

General Tillet further explained. "Yes sir, and the classified activities under the WEBMAZE umbrella program encompass multiple compartments dedicated to different Soviet—now Russian—and Chinese satellites. Of course, the Russians have transitioned to sophisticated encrypted data links, but NSA has always been able to decrypt them. We can have a team inserted in two weeks to perform the signals intercept and possibly control Cosmos 2455 in six weeks or less."

"Haven't the Russians figured out by now that we can control their satellites?" asked Marr.

"Yes sir. They have always suspected that we are capable of controlling their satellites," answered the general. "But we are much more sophisticated now than we were in 1978. We can upload viruses and worms as well as lock out Russian control. We can even make it appear that the satellite is acting erratically due to a solar storm or sun spots."

"I want to know what this satellite is all about before I approve anything, let alone controlling it. If Cosmos 2455 is in fact a weapon system, I want to know what kind of weapon it is and whether or not to destroy it— clandestinely or otherwise. Keep me informed of your progress. This meeting is adjourned!" President Marr got up and then pointed to Generals Tillet and Hollaway and said, "Don't fail."

General Tillet immediately called General Joe Black, head of WEBMAZE Special Operations, on an office Secure Terminal Equipment set that allowed him to discuss classified information. It was General Black, then a captain, who learned how to control Soviet satellites. And General Black knew which team to assign to this dangerous and complex mission.

In his office, General Black opened a safe marked *TOP SECRET / Personnel Records* in large red letters. The specialized telemetry intercept team required a strong and experienced team leader, a communications and intercept receiver expert, a satellite and orbital mechanics expert, two Delta Force special ops sergeants, and an in-country CIA operative. He needed at least two DoD members fluent in Russian. The general flipped open each personnel folder jacket and scanned them:

Steve Walker, Lieutenant Colonel (O-6), US Army
DOB 25 Nov 1979
Commissioned: 2nd Lt (O-1); 14 June 2001 Military Academy at West Point
SOCOM; Ranger Qualified; CMF 18A/18O/35O
Combat Operations – Afghanistan; ODA-Alpha Team Leader; CIA Field Operations Training
Languages (fluent): Russian and French, MBA Boston University
WEBMAZE — Operation Juiquan 2015 / Crimea Operation 2016 / Operation Plesetsk 2017 (Team Leader)

Susan P. MacDonald (aka Mac), Civilian Contractor
DOB 9/12/1989
Principal Scientist; Lincoln Labs; PhD Orbital Mechanics, MIT; CIA Field Operations Training
WEBMAZE — Operation Juiquan 2015 / Crimea Operation 2016 / Operation Semnan 2016 (Tech Lead)

Brian G. Mathers, Captain (O-3), US Air Force
DOB 10/29/1992
Commissioned (AFROTC): 2nd Lt (O-1); 19 May 2014
SOCOM; AFSOC; AFSC 13SX/14NX/17DX; BS & MS EE, NJIT; AF ROTC; CIA Field Operations Training
Specialist: Signal Intercept and Communication Technology
Languages (fluent): German and Spanish

*WEBMAZE — Operation Juiquan 2015 / Crimea
Operation 2016 / Operation Sohae 2016
Operation Sohae-2 2017 (Comm Lead)*

*Jared D. Stone (aka JD), Sergeant (E-5), US Army
DOB 1/4/1994
Enlisted: PVT (E-1); 10 July 2014
SOCOM; 1st SFOD-Delta; MOS 18B/18C/89B/89D;
CIA Field Operations Training
Languages (fluent): French and Spanish
WEBMAZE — Operation Plesetsk 2017*

*Rick Guerrier, Staff Sergeant (E-6), US Army
DOB 3/15/1991
Enlisted: PVT (E-1), 18 Oct 2009
SOCOM; 1st SFOD-Delta; MOS 18B/18C/18F/89B/89D;
CIA Field Operations Training
Languages (fluent): Russian and German
WEBMAZE — Crimea Operation 2016 / Operation
Sohae 2016 / Operation Plesetsk 2017*

*Vladimir Ivanov, Native of Kazakhstan
DOB 5/10/1976
CIA Operative (Civilian) – Recruited in 2008 (Son
killed in Chechen Resistance)
Residence: Baikonur, Kazakhstan / Race Horse Farm
CIA Operations: Operation Poppy Field 2011 (Raid
poppy growers); Operation Big Dome 2013 (assist
CIA operations access to Baikonur Cosmodrome);
Operation Big Sky 2015 (assist CIA with insurgent
infrastructure)*

General Black had his team. They would be contacted
and assembled immediately.

3

THE TEAM HAD made it through the night, Susan dealing with the crude living arrangements, Walker planning the next move, and Brian cooking breakfast. Walker could not talk on the satphone for fear of being intercepted. The satphone had a message burst mode that he could employ, but only on the hour and half hour so that the message appeared to be a centrally controlled UTC time mark. The messages were similar to text messages but only 120 characters.

Walker's first message: *Team safe @ storage facility Waiting orders.* The special ops comm center at the Pentagon received the message and forwarded it to General Black, who immediately replied, *Resume mission Immediate threat unk Team may be compromised.*

General Black had learned from an NSA intercept just prior to mission go-time that a high-level Russian agent had been warned about his team's existence and possibly its mission. There was a mole inside the WEBMAZE team and Black had no idea who it could be.

The WEBMAZE Program was highly compartmented with only a few staffers read into all the code-worded compartments: *CROSSHATCH*, which was satellite performance and analysis, *DEPRESSION*, which was developing the satellite control system, and *AQUADUCT*, which collected the target satellite signals—this was where Walker's team fell.

General Black had to find the mole while his team was on the run. His first decision: close-hold all of the team's plans and actions. Only he would communicate with them from that point forward. He knew they could operate as an independent field team. They had the best chance of completing the mission and getting out of Kazakhstan. It was late, so he decided to sleep at his office, where the satphone feed came through a special circuit set up just for him.

Walker read the message and revealed it to the team. He trusted General Black, but he knew there was more to the situation. The mission had nearly gone bust with all of their lives in jeopardy. *Who else knew where we were and when we would be there?*

Walker's plan revolved around getting back to their hotel in Baikonur, regrouping, and preparing for an evening rerun. "The boss wants us to reengage tonight and expects us to collect more data. JD, Rick—get the cars and bring them around front. Mac, Brian—gather up your gear and load the cars," he said. "Vladimir, we need you to go to the Sputnik Hotel and check if there are any suspicious looking people waiting for us there."

The Sputnik Hotel was typically used by space company reps and the press, so intelligence agents would be fairly easy to spot. Jared and Rick were back with the cars in minutes and loading up Susan's and Brian's gear, but Vladimir froze, rethinking his part of the plan.

"I would prefer to use a disguise before I show up there. Too many people know my face around town. I have disguises at the farm—the farmhands will not get suspicious if I show up and then leave. Someone needs to drop me off and pick me up later."

Walker agreed; Vladimir's judgment in this type of situation was usually good. The team's undercover identities as "real estate investors" required training to fill roles as land surveyors, property value analysts, advertisers and, of course, buyers; all might now be in jeopardy.

"If it's okay with you, boss, I'll drive Vladimir to his ranch," Jared said. Walker agreed.

"Okay, just be careful not to draw attention. Brian, get your stuff out of Jared's Fiesta and put it in Rick's."

Before the rest of the team squeezed into Rick's Fiesta, Walker yelled, "Let's all meet up at the Café Svesdnoe Nevo on Arbat street at 1500. It's got pretty good food!"

"I hope we don't have to eat horse meat," Susan huffed.

They drove off, Jared to Vladimir's ranch and Rick to the center of Baikonur where the plan was to hide in plain sight. When they arrived at a shopping area in the center of Baikonur, Walker suggested they split up to draw less attention.

"Mac, you stay with me. Brian, you go with Rick."

Since Rick and Walker both knew Russian, they could walk the streets and buy souvenirs at nearby shops. After a few hours of walking around shopping, at 1445 local they all descended on the café and waited for Vladimir and Jared to show up.

4

VLADIMIR SHOWED UP at the café at exactly 1500 dressed like a university professor with a wig, beard, and mustache. The hat and tweed jacket were a nice touch. The only giveaway was Jared following closely behind. Vladimir looked a bit disheveled, and Rick said, in Russian, "You look like an absent-minded professor."

Susan was impressed by how good the disguise was and remarked, "You can't tell it's you in there. Amazing transformation!"

Vladimir had a little more confidence now. "Why, thank you, madam!"

Walker said, "Scope out the hotel and, if possible, check out our rooms. Prepping for the mission will be easier there. Besides, we all need a shower and a change of clothes."

"Amen to that," Susan said.

They read the menu and, unfortunately for Susan, horse and lamb were the primary offerings. Walker and Vladimir constantly scanned the customers at the café. It would be a disaster to get called out by FSB agents in public. To lower suspicion, Vladimir and Walker spoke in Russian, which drove the rest of the team nuts—except Rick, who barely kept up. Susan was almost finished with her mutton dinner when she requested some baursaki, which was fried dough, and dates. She liked to cook and was fascinated by Kazakh breads, sweet biscuits and snack bars.

When they were almost finished eating, Vladimir said to Walker, "I'll drive the Fiesta to the Sputnik Hotel alone and call you on your cell phone whether it is safe or not. If it is, I will stay there, and we can meet at the hotel. If the FSB is there, what should I do?"

Walker was a bit hesitant. "If the FSB is there, we'll regroup at the alternate site. We must execute tonight!"

The alternate site was a dilapidated bus station no longer used by local workers going to and from the cosmodrome. This was Vladimir's second choice because it was close to the road but a little further from the cosmodrome than the farmhouse. There would be an issue hiding the cars, but Vladimir had a solution for that. As for the other issue, an escape route, there was no solution.

"First go to the storage facility outside of town and wait there for me," Vladimir said. After he drove off, the rest of the team went to Vladimir's backup hideout and waited for his call. Walker knew that there was a third possibility—Vladimir could be captured, which would really screw everything up. He needed to be prepared for that possibility.

Vladimir arrived at the hotel, and based on the number of cars parked there, it did not appear to be busy. He checked his disguise for the last time and went into the lobby. He looked around and saw nothing suspicious, then went up to a female receptionist and spoke in Russian.

"I am Professor Lubichenkov from the University. What is your daily rate?"

"Hello, Professor. Our daily rate is 26,600 rubles."

"May I please see what the rooms are like? My wife is very finicky and needs a quiet room with a soft bed."

The receptionist called for someone to assist the professor and then rolled her eyes. A young girl in her twenties came and the receptionist said, "Please show the professor some rooms and answer any questions he may have."

"What kind of room are you looking for?" the girl asked.

"A nice quiet room with all the amenities for me and my wife. We'll be staying here next weekend."

As they approached the final hallway, no one appeared suspicious. Vladimir saw only some men in suits heading out to their cars, probably for an afternoon of heavy drinking.

The girl showed Vladimir a few rooms and he nodded in approval. He and the girl strolled down the final hallway, where Walker's team had stayed in four of the rooms. Two of the rooms had open doors with clothing strewn all over the floor. He saw no sign of the FSB agents who must have searched them. Vladimir and the girl returned to the lobby.

"I think my wife would like this place," he told the receptionist. "Do you have rooms available for the following weekend?"

"Yes, of course. Would you like to reserve now?"

Not having ID for his professor role, Vladimir said, "Not at the moment; I will call my reservation in this week." Vladimir recorded the Sputnik's telephone number and said, "Thank you for the tour. You have been most helpful."

As Vladimir started toward the exit, he didn't see the young man dressed in all black leather with boots to match who entered the lobby from around a corner. The man walked slowly behind Vladimir and followed him through the exit door and then to the small, remote lot where Vladimir had parked the Fiesta. Vladimir knew he was being followed; he heard the boots hitting the pavement. He guessed his pursuer was either an FSB agent or a thief planning to rob him. He hoped it was a thief, who he could easily dispatch with his Baikal 441 pistol.

The young man called out, in Russian, "Can you please tell me where the nearest restaurant is?" Vladimir pulled out his pistol, then turned. The young man had pulled out a Taser and Vladimir beat him to the draw, shooting the man twice in the chest. The man fell to the ground and stopped moving a few seconds later. Vladimir checked for a pulse as he scanned the area for witnesses and then dragged the dead man behind the Fiesta.

He found an FSB ID in his wallet along with some other official-looking government papers. *Der'mo! This is really bad*, he thought. *I've just killed an FSB agent in broad daylight! I must report back to the team, now.*

Vladimir struggled to load the body into the trunk and drove off. He immediately called Walker on his cell phone and explained what had happened

"I'm okay, but we cannot go back to the Sputnik. An FSB agent was about to Taser me, so I had no choice but to shoot. There were no witnesses that I could see. It also appeared that the FSB has been in your rooms!"

"Go back to your ranch, ditch the disguise, hide the body in the woods after dark and then meet us at the alternate site at 2100," Walker ordered. "Call me only if things go sideways. You good with that?"

"Yes, understood."

Vladimir knew what he had to do. Walker was right. It wouldn't be long before other FSB agents swarmed the Sputnik.

Walker related the negative turn of events to the team. "Vladimir was shadowed by an FSB agent and unfortunately he had to shoot him. He's pretty sure there were no witnesses. We're meeting him at the abandoned bus terminal tonight at 2100. So, no showers or clean clothes tonight."

So much for hotel life, Walker thought.

Vladimir followed the plan, dumping the FSB agent's body deep in the woods, and waited at his ranch.

5

THE TEAM, ALL five with their hardware, crammed into the Fiesta and arrived a few minutes before nine that night at the old bus station. The Fiesta was packed like a sardine with Jared, Brian, and Rick squeezed together in the back seat.

"Good thing we didn't have to share a lap," Brian joked.

"That's why Mac is sitting up here with me," Walker said.

Susan laughed. "Sorry, no free lap dances on this ride!"

"We better dismount now," Jared said. "I'm about to cut the cheese." With that, they all jumped out of the car.

They could barely see the lights of the cosmodrome antenna farm from the ground floor.

"We haven't heard from Vladimir, so he must have either taken care of business or got caught," Walker said.

Just then, a Fiesta slowly approached. The lights flashed twice, then went dark. Walker flashed his flashlight at the Fiesta three times. The car came to a stop behind the other Fiesta and Vladimir emerged. He seemed awfully calm to Walker, who asked, "You okay?"

"I did what I had to do." Vladimir cautioned the team, "Guards will be periodically driving up and down the main street checking for intruders and possibly homeless people. Military patrols are typically active within a mile of the main building complex and seldom do sweeps outside the perimeter fence. I brought something to hide the cars. Bring both vehicles together in a V formation on the left side of the building."

"JD, Rick—get the cars," Walker ordered.

Jared and Rick drove onto the grass and parked in a V as instructed. Vladimir took a black tube out of his Fiesta, then pulled out a rolled-up cloth, unfurled it and pulled out a bunch of skinny steel rods and assembled what eventually looked like the front and sides of a small storage shed. At a distance, it looked real.

"This is how the Russians defeated the Germans in WWII, by making it appear we had more weapons than we really had," said Vladimir, who was a collector of WWII paraphernalia and bought the fake shed at a military surplus store in Saint Petersburg.

"Pretty impressive. I hope it works," said Walker. "JD, Rick, move Vladimir's shed into position and get the equipment from the Fiestas. Carry it to the back door of the bus terminal."

Everyone else waited while Walker picked the lock. "Use light discipline and use only the red headlights," he said.

Locking the door behind him, Walker and the team quickly went to the top floor, stairs creaking with every step. Brian set up the antennas and receiving equipment. Telemetry data from Cosmos 2455 and the cosmodrome would be collected on Brian's laptop and eventually correlated to Cosmos 2455 maneuvers.

Jared and Rick had set up their miniature temblor sensors outside to warn of intruders while they waited for Vladimir to arrive. Originally developed to support special ops infiltration, these high-tech units were developed to easily plant in soil or stick to any surface. Their status was monitored on both JD's and Rick's specially modified smartphones. Meanwhile, Cosmos 2455 broke the horizon and Susan called out, "Satellite on the horizon!" About five minutes later, Brian noted satellite signals and started the recording process—collecting both satellite and control tower signals.

"Stay on your toes," Walker ordered. "JD, Rick, watch for any intruders!"

Data was collected successfully as the satellite passed. If this data collection had failed, they would have had to wait for a second pass in about an hour and forty minutes, doubling the risk of getting caught. Unfortunately, the team would not know if Lacrosse was also successfully monitoring the satellite's maneuvers until much later.

"Satellite and ground telemetry terminated!" Susan declared. "Cosmos 2455 is OTH!"

"Outstanding!" called Walker. "Break it down, pack it up and let's get the hell out of here."

6

DEEP IN THE bowels of Lubyanka Square was the FSB counterintelligence headquarters. There, a telephone conversation grew out of control between the head of the Counter-Intelligence Directorate, Director Vasilly Arkonov, and a woman speaking perfect English on the other end.

"Your intelligence was flawed, and after a thorough search of the farmhouse, nothing was found! We pay you a lot of money to get it right!"

"There's no doubt that the team was there that night!" the woman insisted. "Did your team look everywhere? What about at the Sputnik? They were registered there for sure; did you find them there?"

"Of course, we looked everywhere including the Sputnik. All we found were rooms of luggage filled with clothing and no trace of their whereabouts! We have stepped up patrols in case they are still in the area. Is there anything new you can tell us about their mission?"

"All contact with the team has been discontinued," the woman said. "Only the general and possibly the comm techs have contact with them now. For all I know, their mission was cancelled, and they could have been recalled."

"Find out what the plan is," the director ordered. "I don't like surprises. Do whatever it takes to get the information."

The director hung up and called the captain.

"Captain, starting at dusk, I want your team to check all the buildings within two miles of the main cosmodrome building, and do it all night long."

"Yes sir. We will start patrolling outside the fenced area in double sweeps. If there is anyone out there, we will find them."

The only people wandering around the gate had been homeless or were opportunists looking for souvenirs to sell in town. But, not wanting to disobey orders, the captain rounded up his men.

"The director wants us to do a thorough search of the grounds outside the fence. If you see anybody, check them out."

At sundown, the captain and his search team drove their GAZ Tigers to the fenced entrance to the cosmodrome, then split up searching the grounds outside the fence in a widening spiral. He and his three men headed south, and the lieutenant and his three men headed north.

The director was expecting a call from one of his younger agents but had not heard from him since the agent called in when he arrived at the Sputnik. The young agent reported that the American spies had been staying at the hotel. The agent was usually reliable about reporting in every hour, so the director was concerned.

The director called the agent on his cell phone but got no response. He decided it was time to send out two agents to look for him—starting with the Sputnik Hotel. This was becoming reminiscent of an operation that went south years ago because the director was not thorough enough. There were too many loose ends and he needed to tighten down the screws.

After hanging up, the woman realized that somehow the team must have found out that they were exposed and aborted the mission. She needed to find the team's whereabouts but would have to wait until she got to work at headquarters. It was five in the morning when she was startled by the telephone call.

Having a WEBMAZE clearance and being part of the AQUADUCT workforce, she was positioned to hear anything relevant to the team's mission. If they had been warned ahead of time, that could mean that her encrypted conversation with the head of Russian counterintelligence at the FSB had been monitored and decrypted by the NSA. That would be impossible to verify since access to NSA intercepts required a different clearance. She would just have to go to work and act as if everything were normal. She felt bad about her betrayal, but the money she was being paid for treason was going to save her mother's life. Besides, the worst that could happen to the team would be to stand trial for espionage but eventually get traded in a spy swap with Russia.

Six o'clock was looming. She needed to get ready for work. As number two on the USAF security team, she had to be there bright and early.

7

WHILE THE TEAM was packing up, Jared called out, "Temblor activity—looks like a few people walking through the temblor zone."

Everybody froze while Jared and Rick went to the window to see what triggered the temblors. The ones near the street triggered first. The temblors closer to the building now showed signs of activity. Jared and Rick saw the outlines of three people carrying what appeared to be AKs.

"Looks like we have three intruders approaching the building," Jared whispered.

"Lights out. Let's wait and see what they do," Walker said. "They might be doing sweeps and move on. If not and they attempt entry, we'll have to take them out. Rick, JD, stay close to the floor entrance. Make sure no one gets away; you three"—pointing to Susan, Brian, and Vladimir—"stay low and behind the old ticket counter. Be absolutely quiet."

Everybody heard the tugging on the door and then multiple attempts to open windows. The sounds were a bit unsettling to hear in the dark. Susan and Brian looked at each other as if to say, *Could things get worse?*

Past ops for her were much easier and less stressful and usually executed at longer distances from the telemetry centers. Susan had an uneasy feeling that something really bad was about to happen. Brian, who was crouched in an uncomfortable squat, decided to shift, but when he did, his miniature receiver fell out of his bag and onto the floor with a thud. Everyone heard it, including the armed intruders, who froze in place. Brian knew he messed up; his heart raced. There was no sound at all for what seemed an eternity, and then the sweep team leader blurted out in Russian, "Probably a stray cat, and who cares anyway? This place is a shithole!"

Jared and Rick were ready to take down the two closest intruders and drill the third. If there were more, it could quickly turn into a shitstorm. Instead, the three men walked off into the distance, never even noticing the fake shed Vladimir had erected.

"Intruders departing. Temblors following," Jared whispered.

"Vladimir, did they say something about cats?" Walker asked.

Vladimir, half laughing, said, "They think we are cats."

"Okay, people, let's get the hell out of here," Walker ordered. "We need to get this data transmitted back to the Center ASAP."

Brian reminded Walker, "We shouldn't set up within intercept range of nearby satcom systems, so we have to get far away from Baikonur. Suggest we head east of Baikonur, far enough from the Krayniy Airport and Tyuratam railway center so no chance of intercepting our data transmission."

"Okay. We'll drive to Baikonur, pick up M32, then drive east toward Dzhusaly. About twenty miles out, there is nothing but dirt and dust."

"All clear," Jared called. "The threat has left."

Everyone got up to leave, and Brian apologized to the team. "Sorry, guys. I got a leg cramp and had to move. That won't happen again."

Vladimir went over to Brian and said, "Those dummies have no idea how smart these cats are!" Jared and Rick chuckled.

Jared and Rick lead the way out of the building, this time with their NVGs on. There was nothing in sight except the low flashing UV lights of the temblors they needed to pick up and turn off. Vladimir followed immediately behind them, walking to the two Fiestas hidden behind his fake shed. Vladimir disassembled it and put it back into its long container. Although she was less stressed, Susan still had an uneasy feeling. It was almost pitch black with a few lights visible at the cosmodrome center.

Susan hadn't drawn a full breath when Jared and Rick blurted out, almost in unison, "Vehicle approaching! We need to get behind the building. Now!"

With the NVGs, they spotted the vehicle's lights over two miles away but approaching fast. Walker was concerned that the people in the oncoming vehicle would see the Fiestas.

"JD, Rick, get the Fiestas behind the building; take up defensive positions on both sides of the building," Walker ordered.

There was no time to replant the temblor sensors so they could keep track of the car from behind cover.

"Brian, Mac, Vladimir, get behind the building and stay between Rick and JD. Let's wait and see what this is all about."

Walker was considering escape routes when, sure enough, the oncoming sedan slowed as it passed by the old bus station. A very bright beam of light shot out from the rear passenger window and flooded the area with light.

The main beam centered on the old bus station's windows and front door. Rick got the first wave in his NVGs and was temporarily blinded. The NVGs were fifth generation, brand new to the DoD, and able to handle UV, IR, low light, and sudden bright lights called "blooms." The flashlight bloom was attenuated in 150 milliseconds and the light source strongly filtered.

Fortunately for the team, the rear seat passenger told the driver to continue. "Nothing here. Go to the next building. I hate these fucking LED flashlights—the beam sucks. What a fucking waste of money."

The driver nodded and said, "What do you care? It's not your money."

As soon as the taillights were dim and distant, the team split up and piled into the Fiestas. They headed south to Baikonur—lights off. The drive was a straight shot along the access road south, then onto M32 heading east toward Dzhusaly. About halfway between the two cities, Brian directed them off the highway and south toward the Syr Darya River.

Once they were far enough away from M32 and could not see any traffic, they drove off the road about fifty yards and parked—lights off. Everyone dismounted while Brian set up his encrypted miniature Inmarsat satcom system and transmitted the gigabyte of data from the intercept. Jared and Rick got the M-107s ready and put on their NVGs and set a crude perimeter. Everyone else stood around while the upload was in progress.

"Is it just me or does it seem like there's a tracking device on the cars?" Susan asked.

Walker explained, "It's just good detective work since we were compromised. No one knows where we are or where we're going now that all our comms go through General Black."

"So, where do we go from here?" asked Susan.

Walker was curt but clear. "Headquarters is getting their data, so they know we're okay. General Black will tell us our next move."

About twenty minutes later, when all the data was uploaded, Walker got an acknowledgement on his satphone. *ALL DATA RCVD; GO TO SH.* The *SH* was the "safe house" operated by the CIA in Dzhusaly—that was further south and east on M32. There were multiple safe houses in the Baikonur area, and they were to be used only for emergencies.

"We're headed to a safe house in Dzhusaly," he said. "Get the equipment loaded and mount up."

Walker and Brian were in Jared's Fiesta and Susan and Vladimir in Rick's. It was another sixty miles, which seemed to take forever on the dark road.

The Dzhusaly safe house was news to Vladimir, who had no idea there was another CIA operation in the area. He asked Rick, "How long has the CIA had this safe house?"

Rick was also clueless. "Got no idea. I suspect that only Colonel Walker knows where they all are."

Susan, a bit surprised, asked, "So, what happens if Colonel Walker is killed or captured? How would the team know about the safe houses?"

"I believe it's protocol with the CIA. It sort of guarantees that safe houses aren't compromised," Rick said.

Vladimir asked Rick the next obvious question. "Are there more safe houses in the area?"

"I don't know, and neither should you."

"So, how long have you been in the spy business?" Susan asked Vladimir.

"Ten years."

"Do you ever worry about being caught?"

"I hope not. I have a great life here, even though I oppose the government. I live comfortably on my horse farm. I raise and train race horses and have a few large

Arabian-style workhorses. I don't think anyone suspects me of being anything other than a horse trainer."

"So, what made you decide to be a spy for the CIA?" Susan persisted.

"Why do you ask that question?"

"I'm just curious why you'd help Americans and go against your country. I mean, you actually killed an FSB agent!"

"When my only son was killed in the Chechen War, they did not want to tell me how he died. I found out later that he was shot in the back by one of his own comrades during a Chechen raid. He was a good commander and wanted to be proud of his team. A few of his comrades had conspired to kill him because his team was usually picked for difficult missions. With the CIA's help, I eventually found out who they were. The CIA secretly got rid of them all. For that, I am grateful. I have never told this to anyone else; you and Rick are the first ones to hear this."

"I'm truly sorry to hear about your son's murder, but now I understand why you do what you do." Susan left that subject alone and started a conversation about race horses—one of Vladimir's favorite topics.

8

THEY ARRIVED AT the safe house located on the southwest edge of Dzhusaly on the Syr Darya River. It was a fairly large house owned by a rich Kazakh business man who rented it for an outrageous sum of ₸741,000 a month, equal to about $4,000 USD. A seven-foot cement wall surrounded the property, and an electronic gate controlled a single access to the grounds. The agents running the safe house remotely monitored and controlled the wall perimeter, including the access gate, 24/7. So as not to be too conspicuous, there were no antennas, sensors, cameras, or weapons visible from the street. To the locals, it looked like a typical resort haven for wealthy Kazakhs.

The agents were waiting for the team when they approached the gate, opening it when the headlights flashed the access code—dot dot dash, dot dot dot, dot dash. Over an intercom near the gate the team heard, "Drive into the open garage door." The agents knew no one was following because a long-range camera on the roof disguised as a weathervane would have detected pursuing vehicles. The team pulled the Fiestas inside a huge nine-car garage fifty feet from the gate.

The garage extended three car lengths, and there were two other cars already inside. The gate and garage door shut automatically behind them. It was well lit for a garage and there were cameras in all four corners. There was no visible door until a storage shelf opened with a beep. Then a person spoke over invisible speakers in broken English. "Lock both cars and bring the keys and all your equipment with you."

"Grab all your stuff and get inside—weapons too," Walker added.

Two young men who spoke perfect English, one with a slight Kazakh accent, greeted the team.

"We've been expecting you and your team, Lieutenant Colonel Walker. My name is Howard, and this is Nuro."

"Thanks. We're exhausted, hungry, and dirty. We'll take care of our special equipment. Can you please store our weapons for us?"

Susan was ecstatic. "Howard, does the safe house have a bath?"

"Yes, of course, and a change of clothes for everyone."

"Seriously? That would be especially amazing since we left all our clothes at the Sputnik. Do you know my size?"

"Of course," answered Howard. "We have everyone's size!"

The general must have taken care of everything, Walker thought.

"I appreciate all of this, Colonel, but I must get back as soon as possible before someone misses me—especially my workers," Vladimir said.

"I understand, but for now we've got to stay here until we get our next orders."

They were each shown their bedroom and closet with clothes their size. Next was the kitchen and where the food and tableware were kept. Howard, the lead agent, showed them where everything was.

"Eat and drink what you want, but please clean up after yourselves. We don't have room service here."

"Where is Nuro?" Walker asked.

"The two of us man this safe house 24/7 and always look for signs of a compromise. He is checking the perimeter monitors and sensors for any intrusions now that you have arrived."

"We're positive that no one followed us, but I can understand your concern," Walker said. He instructed the team to get some sleep and be ready to move out in the morning.

Susan planned to eat a light snack and then take a bath; Vladimir headed to his bedroom with Brian in tow. Jared and Rick both got some cold cuts and made sandwiches. Walker contacted command center and acknowledged their arrival at the safe house. After he left the STE room, Walker went to Howard and requested a wake-up at 0700. He asked that everyone else be awakened by 0800, then he found his room and settled in for a few hours' sleep. It was now after 0300 and lights-out at the compound. All the auto-alert sensors were activated.

Director Arkonov was getting more concerned that one of his star agents never checked in. The cosmodrome sweeps he ordered came up empty, but he believed the officer-in-charge did his best. He said to himself, "That American bitch better come through; my neck is on the line." He had already assigned FSB agents to look for the American team trying to leave the country at border crossings, airports, and train stations. Based on rental data, he knew he was looking for two Fiestas—but that was hours ago.

9

A FEW MINUTES after Cosmos 2455 passed over Baikonur, it approached the *Yuriy Ivanov* spy ship. The vessel was the latest of Russia's signals intelligence collection ships. Long gone were the covert converted fishing trawlers of the 1960s.

In addition to the signal intercept antennas and radios, the ship was outfitted for a special mission. As it cruised south at a modest five knots in the Sea of Okhotsk, the special test crew members prepared for the fifteenth in a series of twenty planned tests. The ship was towing a very large array of sixteen interconnected mini-barges— each with an antenna and radio suite covering the comm spectrum from HF to SHF. Invisible due to their smaller size were antennas specifically for GPS, Iridium, Inmarsat, and cell phones. Each mini-barge had a communication datalink cable directly connected to the ship from each radio. Each side of the four-by-four array was almost 100 yards, with each barge measuring approximately fifteen yards on each side.

The ship's captain was told by the test team leader to maintain five knots on the current heading. The team leader then yelled to the data collection crew, "Cosmos is in view. Be prepared to track and monitor. The test will begin in a few minutes."

After about ten minutes, the team leader announced over the intercom, "Test has ended. Signals analysis status please!"

The test team's lead engineer responded over the intercom, "The test was a success. With output power of around five percent sustained through the pass, the focus was centered and maintained on the inner four platforms."

That was considered a better pass than the previous fourteen, during which stray radiation hit the outer barges.

"The radios affected by the high-powered microwaves were the VHF through EHF, but the rest seemed to be unaffected," the engineer said. That confirmed what the HPM scientists had been saying all along: not all radios or frequencies would be affected by the HPM directed energy weapon—even with a concentrated beam.

Energy had been accurately deposited in the same small area while the ship was moving at five knots and the satellite sped overhead at 17,500 miles per hour.

"Test completed. Shut everything down and get ready for tomorrow night's test. I'll call in the results to headquarters," the team leader called out. "Captain, reverse course and return to the starting position for tomorrow night's test."

The ship went dark except for the helm. There was a seventy-mile return leg that would take almost seven hours dragging sixteen barges through two and three-foot waves. This was the most sophisticated electronic sensor ship in Russia, but its captain never thought it would be towing barges. Under his breath he blurted, *"Der'mo"*— *shit* in Russian.

Director Arkonov was impatient—and frustrated. With the escape of the US intercept team, his best agent's whereabouts unknown, and the wait to hear from his "WEBMAZE" mole—all within sixty hours—he felt like he was not in control. It was time to chat with his mole to find out more about the team's location. He dialed her burner phone. She picked up and said, "I will call you back at the alternate number in two minutes," and then hung up.

The director suspected something was wrong, so he walked briskly to a landline phone in a conference room where, fortunately, no one was meeting. Two minutes passed, then three, then four and then the phone finally rang. The director, not one for chitchat, got right to it.

"So, what the hell is going on?"

"I think the NSA is somehow monitoring your telephone!" she said nervously. "I think that's how the team knew they were compromised. I'm calling you on a burner phone that I'll be destroying after I hang up. We need to set up a new means of communicating. I may also be compromised depending on how good the NSA is— and they're pretty good. I haven't learned anything new about the team, but I believe they're still in-country. I'll call you at this number tomorrow at the same time with a new burner. I don't want to arouse suspicion by asking too many questions at this time."

The director, a bit pissed off that his well-paid mole was calling the shots, countered with, "I understand your situation, but you need to press harder to find out where they are. You get paid a lot of money because you are valuable to us—so get their status!"

"I will have more for you tomorrow." She hung up and immediately destroyed the phone. She thought, *Holy shit! I hope there's no video of my burner phone purchases at the local pharmacy!*

10

UNDER SECRETARY OF Defense Sheffield called a meeting to get a status update on the intercept mission. He requested WEBMAZE head General Black, CIA director Greenway, NSA director Duffy, USAF chief of staff General Holloway, and USSTRATCOM's General Tillet to brief him on Cosmos 2455. Before everyone got seated, Sheffield asked, "So, where are we with the SIGINT of Cosmos 2455?"

General Black spoke first. "Sir, my team was inserted and ready to collect when I got a call from the WEBMAZE detachment at the NSA."

Director Duffy nodded and followed with, "Sir, we intercepted a telephone call to a high-level FSB cell phone assigned to the counterintelligence unit. Our SIGINT team determined it was from a woman here in the States. It took only a few minutes to decrypt the telephone call because they used a simple commercial encryption algorithm. Unfortunately, we couldn't trace the call since it was routed through too many nodes. However, we know it was from somewhere in the eastern US and that it was a burner phone. But we now have her voiceprint. It was clear that she was giving away the intercept location of the AQUADUCT team—at which time I immediately called General Black."

"And I had to wave off the team immediately via satphone," Black said. "And after they recovered, they went back last night to re-engage the SIGINT mission. They were successful and already uploaded the SIGINT data from their 1000 local overpass."

General Tillet spoke next. "Sir, we have good news. We were able to visibly monitor Cosmos 2455 through the same time period and we can correlate the satellite's response to the uplinked commands and downlinked responses. The noticeable increase in satellite footprint was striking; it nearly tripled in size and had a significant onboard temperature increase as monitored with infrared."

Sheffield pressed. "So, what does all this mean? Is it a weapon system or not?"

Tillet said brusquely, "Unfortunately, sir, with only one collection and one correlation to satellite motion, that's not enough to make a determination. However, we don't believe the Russians know we can perform that level of visualization from an MEO telescopic satellite system. We suspect the increase in size may allow for an increase in electronic beam focus and amplitude, which would be ideal for a—"

Sheffield interrupted, "A weapon system?"

"Possibly, or possibly a specialized communication intercept system," Tillet said.

"So, what's next?" asked Sheffield.

"Sir, my team is waiting for orders; no one communicates with them except me," General Black said. "Until we learn the source of the compromise, that's the only way it can work. They're presently at the CIA safe house in Dzhusaly."

Sheffield looked concerned. "They should stay there until we need a follow-up action. President Marr wants to know as much as possible about this satellite."

Tillet added, "Sir, later in orbit, the satellite returns to its smaller footprint. We need to reposition the reconnaissance MEO so that we can monitor both the Baikonur datalink maneuvers of Cosmos 2455 and the approximate location in orbit where it shrinks back to normal. We plan to start the maneuvers this morning."

Sheffield pointed at CIA director Greenway and said, "Find the mole. We can't have traitors compromising our operations!"

Greenway responded, "Sir, it's already in motion. We contacted Gordon Daniels, and as the DNI he tasked the FBI. We'll find her."

"That'll be all, gentlemen. Get to work."

General Black contacted Lieutenant Colonel Walker the following morning on the safe house STE.

"The WEBMAZE tech team was able to correlate Captain Mathers's SIGINT data to Cosmos 2455's physical expansion, but they need more data," General Black said. "Your team must execute additional intercepts to figure this out. We've briefed the president, who now believes that Cosmos 2455 may actually be a weapon system."

"Sir, we almost got discovered at the farmhouse when you called. We escaped with seconds to spare," Walker said. "When Vladimir went back to the Sputnik, he saw that our rooms had been rifled through. Someone obviously knew we were there. Then there's Vladimir's killing an FSB agent in self-defense!"

"I knew with a mole in the loop you guys were in for a shitstorm," the general said. "If you and your team are up to the task, we'll need more signal intercepts over the next week or so. Is your team ready to continue the op?"

Walker couched his response. "Sir, Susan and Brian aren't trained for combat ops, but I know they'll do whatever it takes. We almost had a run-in with a sweep team at an abandoned bus station, but lucky for us, they kept moving. We've got weapons, ammo, and food, but Susan said she needs a data drop to support the Cosmos 2455 updated ephemeris. I'll put the question to the team and let you know where we are. We got a good night's sleep, so should be ready for tonight's tasking. Walker out."

"I'll have Callahan's team send the updated ephemeris data right now. Let me know if you need anything else. Center out."

11

AT THE SAFE house, the team looked to Lieutenant Colonel Walker to establish their next move. Jared popped the question everyone wanted the answer to.

"So, boss, what's our next move? We still in the game or not?"

"Did they figure out who the mole is yet?" Susan asked.

Vladimir's concern was about his ranch. "My unexplained absence will be problematic if it extends beyond three days. The staff may get nervous and call the *politsiya* and file a missing person report. I must also get back by the end of the week to pay the workers their wages."

Brian, Jared and Rick understood well the chain-of-command and trusted Walker's leadership style, which was more like a supervisor than a commander. He never needed to raise his voice—except once, when on a special ops mission, someone had used their cell phone to call home. That person was ejected from the team.

"The mole is being flushed out, the satellite situation is evolving, and, unless something really big intervenes, we're probably going back tonight," Walker said. "And yes, we're in FSB crosshairs, but as long as we avoid them, we'll be okay. Mac, you okay if we go back tonight? We really need your expertise out there. General Black will give us our orders when he gets up later today. I'm sure he had a long night coordinating with the other teams."

"Well, I signed up for this, and so far we have successfully evaded the FSB. I guess I'm still in," Susan said.

"Great!" Walker said. "Oh, you should be getting an updated ephemeris in the next thirty minutes via SIPR. Head over to the STE room. Vladimir, call your head ranch hand and let him know you're gonna be away on business and should be back by the weekend."

Walker was careful not to mention WEBMAZE because neither of the safe house agents was read in. "We'll have to ditch the Fiestas because by now the FSB is looking for them."

"We have three grey Lada Vesta sedans—all made in 2017," Howard said. "They are so common that no one will notice them. They're solid, safe, and fairly reliable—and oh, did I mention that no one will notice them?"

"We'll take you up on that offer since we'll need to blend in even more with the FSB looking for anything out of the ordinary."

The woman on the other end of the line was stressed. "All indications are that the team appears to still be there. But we were told that starting tomorrow the staff will be given lie detector tests, and they didn't explain why. I'm sure it's to find the mole within the WEBMAZE program. They usually do the security staff last, but with everyone else, it's alphabetical by last name. They will probably get to me in three days! I don't know what to do."

Director Arkonov was prepared. "Just lie about everything they ask, then fake a breakdown saying that you lied because you told your mother about the work you do there. Or you can tell them the truth—that you needed five hundred thousand for your mother's illegal kidney transplant surgery. Then, of course, you will stand trial for treason, be convicted, and go to jail for twenty-five years. I would go with option one."

"But what if I decide to come clean and tell them I'm the mole and give you up?"

"I thought I made it perfectly clear," said the director. "I will have your mother killed, but it will look like an accident. We have already paid you three hundred thousand for your services, but if you give yourself up, your mother's surgery was a waste of time."

She silently weighed her options. "I will call you tomorrow night, same time."

She was first contacted when a nice British fellow bumped into her at a small nearby café five months back. He knew her name, where she worked, and that her mother needed a kidney transplant. It all seemed so easy at first, supplying classified information about WEBMAZE, but when the AQUADUCT team went to Kazakhstan and the Russians asked for their names with pictures, she realized she was in over her head.

"I'm fried either way," she said aloud. "The Russians own me, and I can't protect myself or my mother."

The STE phone rang in the safe house conference room. Nuro answered.

"Line is secure. This is Nuro."

On the other end, General Black said, "Put Colonel Walker on the phone."

Walker answered. "Sir, we are go for tonight if you need us."

"An interesting development with the satellite may require your team to collect satellite signals further along in the orbit. Satellite imagery shows Cosmos 2455 appearing to expand in size by a factor of three as it passes over Baikonur and then collapsing back to normal a little later in the orbit. Do you have enough data storage for an extended collection? We need Captain Mathers to collect until the telemetry stops with the satellite."

"Sir—can do!" Walker said. "Brian's computer can process and store five times the typical overpass data. By the way, Susan thanks the home team for the updated Cosmos ephemeris data; all received."

"Good luck! Make sure the satphone is fully operational—just in case. Center out."

"Roger that, sir. Out."

The Cosmos 2455 ephemeris data had been received on the safe house SIPRNet computer. Susan downloaded it onto her special laptop. She noticed that the orbit was more elliptical and had a perigee over the Sea of Okhotsk, which lasted only a few minutes before building an apogee prior to crossing Alaska. Susan immediately searched for Walker and found him in the kitchen.

"The satellite hits perigee over the Sea of Okhotsk and then climbs toward apogee over Alaska. I suspect the satellite is doing something over the Sea of Okhotsk and resets before crossing Alaska."

"Let's get General Black back on the phone and let him know." They called General Black on the STE and Susan explained.

"General Black, I suspect there is something happening over the Sea of Okhotsk that might be of interest."

"We can monitor the satellite closely as it crosses over the Sea of Okhotsk, but maybe we can see if there is anything of interest in the water as well. Excellent observation, Susan. I will pass this info on to the other WEBMAZE teams. Good luck tonight."

"Yes sir. Thank you, sir."

General Black coordinated with the NRO to re-task the imagery satellite and use their high-resolution ground and sea mapping to scan the Sea of Okhotsk. He hoped Susan's instincts were correct, since every re-tasking used up precious orbit-maneuvering fuel that could not be replaced. Unfortunately, the conversation with the NRO director did not end well; a high-resolution mapping satellite could not be re-tasked to cover the Sea of Okhotsk until a week later—too late for correlating signal data.

General Black's only remaining option was a high-altitude pass with a Lockheed U-2S reconnaissance aircraft based in Japan. The risk of using a U-2 was that if tracked, it could be shot down, creating an international incident. He contacted the reconnaissance office in Japan immediately via STE and spoke with Colonel Jim "Buzz" Lighthart.

"Hey, Buzz, hope all is well at your command."

"Sir, to what do I owe the pleasure?"

"Let me get right to the point. I need reconnaissance coverage over the Sea of Okhotsk between 1100 and 0100 local tonight. I can't give you all the details, but I need your guy to map everything on the water and I'll need the file by tomorrow at noon. Can you do it?"

"General, the only concern may be a few Russian S-75 Dvina parked along the Russian mainland. Our latest U-2S has stealth at high altitude and a new decoy system, but we don't know how effective it is in operation. How important is this flyover mission, anyway?"

"Buzz, I can say without exaggeration it's one of our most critical missions to date. It involves national security."

"Roger that, General. I'll get the team spooled up and ready for tonight's mission. I'll call when the mission's complete."

"Buzz, I really appreciate your support on this. Good luck to your pilot tonight."

"Sir, I'll contact you when the bird lands."

The U-2S Dragon Lady, named for the secret program's code name, was outfitted with a side-looking radar, or SLR, an electro-optical and infrared camera, also referred to as EO/IR, and a threat warning system. A single pilot operated the aircraft and onboard surveillance systems at altitudes above 70,000 feet MSL. But even at that altitude, it was highly vulnerable. Although the SLR could easily spot the equivalent of a metal rowboat at that altitude, it generated a significant electromagnetic signature that could give its identity away. Thus, the EO/IR option would be used for the search.

Scanning technology had improved the EO/IR sensor's performance and would dwell only on scans detecting a preset object's size and signature. After a few comms with the control tower, the cleared-for-takeoff was issued to the U-2S pilot, who started rolling down the runway at Kadena. It was airborne in a few seconds, going nearly vertical in its climb before heading north to the Sea of Okhotsk.

The U-2S pilot started his EO/IR scan from the outside in (east to west), reducing the risk of detection until near the end of the mission. After two passes covering nearly half the sea surface, the system picked up an unusual shape. It looked like a large ship pulling a matrix of barges. To get a better look, the U-2 pilot descended to 50,000 feet and rescanned the objects, looking for both EO and

IR signatures. Each of the sixteen barges appeared to have multiple heat sources—each one similar to the heat signature from a transmitter. It was the weirdest heat signature the pilot had ever seen.

Just as he was turning back for a second pass, the heat signature jumped five levels, as if somebody turned on a heater. Even more weird was the way the high heat signature jumped from the center of the matrix to one corner, and then the opposite corner, dwelling in each location for thirty seconds. Then, as quickly as it came, the heat signature went back to multiple low-level heat sources, leaving the center and outside corner heat signatures much lower than before.

The U-2S pilot radioed back via satellite datalink what he had seen and captured. He was told to immediately return to base for a technical debrief. He hoped that all the recording equipment worked as advertised—and, of course, that no one had seen him on radar.

12

LIEUTENANT COLONEL WALKER'S team was back on the road in the two Lada Vestas, which actually offered a stiffer ride than the Fiestas. Rick drove the first one with Walker and Susan. Jared drove the other with Brian and Vladimir.

"These damn cars seem to find every bump in the road," Susan groused. "Are the shock absorbers adjustable?"

Rick laughed. "It's Russian; they're not known for their comfort."

Jared, Brian, and Vladimir followed closely but, in the dark, did not notice that Rick was doing his best to avoid the cracks and potholes that had formed over the winter.

"We'd better get a move on," Susan said. "The satellite will be coming over the horizon in less than two hours."

The trip on M32 was uneventful, even at the dirt-road entrance to the cosmodrome. Walker noticed it first. "There's a helicopter ahead with a searchlight! You see it, Rick?"

"Yes sir, and we're on an open road with few buildings, but it seems to be flying toward the northwestern corner of the drome."

Sure enough, the helicopter was flying away from their position, so Rick stepped on it and managed to get to the old bus station in a few minutes. They pulled off the road in front of the station.

Walker was deciding what they should do with the cars when a bright light flashed overhead. It seemed to originate above the clouds and immediately got everyone's attention.

"Did anyone see that?"

Susan and Rick both chimed in, "Yes!" Then Susan said, "And what the hell was it?"

"Did anybody hear anything?" Walker asked.

Susan and Rick both said, in unison, "No."

"That much light without a corresponding noise is produced by airborne photographic lighting systems." Walker jumped out of the Lada and looked up. The source of the light was a six-prop drone at about 3,000 feet and moving south toward M32. It flashed again about 600 yards down the road. If someone was taking pictures, Walker was certain they saw both cars.

Walker said in a calm voice, "They're looking for two Fiestas—not two Ladas. Leave the two cars parked in the street, one with the hood up and its emergency flasher on so it appears disabled."

"Roger that," said Rick as he turned on the flashers and raised the hood.

"What's going on?" Jared asked, stepping out of his vehicle.

Rick explained, "Boss's order. Park closely behind my car."

The team members quickly carried their gear to the bus station. Walker hoped that the drone didn't have a download datalink, which would give them the delay needed to escape undetected. After the close calls last time, Walker used some precaution while breaking back into the bus station.

"JD, Rick. Plant the temblors, then help with the equipment. I'll check out the building."

He checked for booby traps, trip wires, video monitors, motion sensors, and a host of other potential monitors before letting everyone in. Once in, Walker proceeded to recheck the stairway and floors for any additional booby traps.

"This is the creepiest place I've ever been during a mission!" Susan complained.

With twenty minutes to spare, they set up all the equipment for the collection mission. Rick and Jared remotely turned on the motion sensors near the cars—as a precaution. They made sure their weapons were ready to go with full magazines and silencers attached. This time, Brian prepared to record the command signals and satellite signals for as long as the signals could be processed.

Brian got the satellite and cosmodrome tracking receivers ready, initialized both satellite and cosmodrome antennas, did a self-test, and waited for Susan to give the word. Everything was going exactly as planned. Susan, now settled into her professional demeanor, said in a low whisper, "Cosmos 2455 coming over the horizon in two minutes."

The collection began when Brian saw the datalink come up from the cosmodrome, followed by datalink signals from the satellite. The satellite-antenna-tracking algorithm was operating perfectly.

While watching the telemetry signal on the monitor, Brian noticed that a different data mode and format had been transmitted during the last few minutes of signal collection from the cosmodrome. The satellite responded

with what appeared to be a calibration signal mode—
something he had seen before from an older Russian
ELINT satellite.

The collection completed, Walker and the team started
breaking down the SIGINT gear. Off in the distance, Walker
saw the flashes again.

"The photo drone is coming this way," he yelled. "Rick,
you and JD get out to the cars—now! Make like you two
are trying to fix the broken Lada. If the drone descends to
get a closer look, I will take it down with my MP-5. If it just
moves on, then we should be okay. Either way, we get into
the Ladas ASAP and get the hell out of here."

As the drone approached the two Ladas, it suddenly
made a right turn and descended to less than 200 feet,
heading directly to the center of the cosmodrome.

"It was either low on battery or it went back to home
base to do a photo download," Walker said. "It doesn't
matter—let's get out NOW!"

They ran to the cars and jumped in. Just as everyone
got settled into the Ladas, they heard a helicopter in the
distance. Then it was two. Walker knew exactly what it was—
the new Ka-52 Alligator with counter-rotating blades and
a veritable arsenal of weapons, as well as a reconnaissance
video pod with low-light, infrared, and night vision. They
were coming right for the two Ladas.

"JD, Rick—grab the 50 cals out of the trunk. Set up on
the roof of the bus station. When I flatten to the ground,
take out both Alligators! Run! Now!" Walker was winging
it, but he figured if anyone could shoot down a helicopter,
it was JD and Rick.

Rick and Jared were long gone with the high-powered
rifles when the first Ka-52 arrived and hovered overhead
with the lead pilot speaking in Russian over a loudspeaker.

"They want us to get out of our cars, get on our knees, and put our hands over our heads!" Walker said.

Susan, Brian, and Vladimir got out of the vehicles and did exactly what they were told. Walker yelled over the helicopter noise, "When I flatten to the ground I want you all to follow suit, got it?" He looked at Susan, who was starting to panic, and then repeated, "Do you understand?" She looked at Walker and nodded.

Walker knew it would be another minute or so before Jared and Rick were in place, magazine locked, bolt pulled, first round in the chamber, and sighted in. He did not know that Rick and Jared had to shoot off a rooftop access padlock to get to the roof, delaying their setup.

The Alligator pilot in charge was told to land and get close to the intruders. Unfortunately for him, in his haste to land he angled his Alligator with its rear exposed to the bus station roof a mere forty yards away. Walker mentally counted two minutes—then went prone on the ground. Brian and Vladimir followed suit, but Susan didn't realize Walker had gone prone.

"Susan! Get down!" Walker yelled.

The Alligator pilots were confused and thought the Americans had not understood their commands. Nothing happened for what seemed like an eternity. Twenty seconds later, the first round was fired, followed by six more in rapid succession. The lead Alligator spun out of control and the second one rolled heavily to the right. When Walker got up, he saw the lead Alligator plow into the ground and then the second Alligator go in a hundred yards away.

"Rick, JD! Get down," he commanded. "We're leaving! Get into the car!"

Rick and Jared flew through the bus station, ran out to the Ladas, threw the 50 cals into the back seat and jumped into Walker's Lada. After a few minutes, the two Alligators were way behind them, smoke billowing into the sky, as the Ladas quickly turned onto M32 headed for Dzhusaly.

Walker was expecting a surface escort for the Alligators, but they must have gotten a late start. He hoped no one would follow them to the safe house. Susan, riding shotgun with Walker, was still taking the whole thing in.

"What the hell made you think Rick and Jared could take down Russian combat helicopters?" she asked.

"This is a first for me," Jared said. "I've never taken out a helicopter before!"

Rick, a bit more confident, said, "I've fired on the older Mi-8s but could never take one down."

The Russians were now looking for two grey Lada Vestas; they would have to abandon them. Brian followed Walker as Walker abruptly turned onto a side road leading to a farmhouse another 200 yards down the road.

Vladimir blurted out to Brian, "I've been here before! I bought two heavy draft workhorse stallions here for my farm a few years ago. I paid a small fortune in rubles!" As Walker's Lada approached the farmhouse, in the distance two more Alligators were flying low along M32. Walker shut off the car lights and Brian followed suit.

Lights came on in the farmhouse as the Ladas pulled up in front of the garage barn. An older couple appeared at the front door dressed in sleeping attire. Vladimir jumped out of Brian's Lada and walked to the stairs leading to the front door. Walker wondered what the hell Vladimir was doing, but a few minutes later they were all inside drinking vodka and black tea with their newfound friends.

Vladimir had obviously made an impression when he bought the two stallions from Andre and Irina Ospanov over two years ago. The team was offered hot tea and slices of Bavarian cream charlotte that Irina baked and sold to the local market. Vladimir explained the late, unannounced visit in Russian.

"I was showing property to the Americans planning to build an international cosmodrome resort in the area when Susan got very sick and threw up."

"I feel better now that I have some food in my stomach," she said.

"Maybe Vodka not so good; you eat crackers and drink tea," Andre said to Susan, motioning to Irina to get some crackers.

Walker was nervous that the Alligators would eventually scour the countryside for the two Ladas. "We're staying just outside Kyzylorda about four hours from here, so we had better be on our way."

Andre protested. "No! You all stay tonight and for breakfast tomorrow."

Vladimir quickly responded. "We accept, but you must accept my gift for your generous hospitality." He took his Rolex Submariner from his wrist and handed it to Andre.

"I cannot accept that for just being a host!" Andre said.

"I insist," said Vladimir, pushing it back into Andre's hand.

Walker quickly followed with, "Thank you for your hospitality, but we still need to move the cars and park them more securely. JD, come with me to move the Ladas."

Once outside, Walker got more animated. "We've got to hide these damn cars, maybe in the barn. We have to upload the satellite data—tonight!"

After parking both cars in the barn, Walker and Jared prepared the data upload. Walker said, "Go get Brian. I'll finish setting up the Inmarsat antenna."

A few minutes later Brian returned with Jared, set up the transmitter, acquired the Inmarsat satellite channel, and got to work uploading the telemetry data.

Walker told Jared, "Go back inside. We don't want to arouse suspicion." Walker then called the safe house to let them know they were all okay and would be there tomorrow morning—assuming all went well tonight.

"Both TASS and RIA Novosti are claiming that two Ka-52 helicopters collided near the cosmodrome tonight," Howard said. "Did your team have anything to do with that?"

"I'll tell you tomorrow when we get back," Walker said. He called General Black on the satphone and, after the usual ident process, explained what had happened—including the shoot-down of the two Alligators.

"Sir, we were caught red-handed and had no options left."

"Steve, be careful; every road leading in or out of Baikonur will have traffic stops with barricades," General Black said. "You and your team should get back to the safe house ASAP. We're processing the intercept telemetry Brian is sending. You should be aware that U-2 surveillance noted some very odd electromagnetic events as the satellite passed overhead."

"That's a strange coincidence," Walker said. "Brian said he noticed the satellite was sending calibration telemetry toward the later phase of signal acquisition. Tonight, we're laying low at a nearby farmhouse, and would you believe Vladimir knows these people?"

"Good thing," General Black said. "Vladimir has friends everywhere. Good luck—keep your team safe. Call me from the safe house tomorrow. Center out."

"Agent out."

Brian finished transmitting the data and broke down the equipment.

"We're almost there! General Black sends his regards."

Walker couldn't share what he knew with Brian or the team just yet. They both went back inside, and Irina Ospanov showed them where their beds were. Walker told Jared and Rick to rotate guard duty and keep an eye on the road—which meant temblors again. Susan was so exhausted she fell asleep right away, but before she did, she snuck a large piece of the Bavarian cream charlotte cake. Vladimir couldn't sleep, so he listened to the Ospanovs' radio in the kitchen. He heard the news about the two helicopters colliding and thought, *That was a really close call. I wonder if they took pictures of us before they went down. I may never be able to go home again!*

13

DUE TO THE Ka-52 pilots' quick thinking, the crews only suffered minor injuries. The head of security at the cosmodrome arrived in a GAZ Tiger along with a small defensive team that established perimeters around the crash sites. Unfortunately, the only video taken of the two Ladas was by the drone—when Jared and Rick were under the hood.

The director of FSB counterintelligence got to the crash site within an hour but was told there was no capture. Each pilot gave a quick description of the occupants of the two grey Ladas—four people, three men and a woman. Director Arkonov pulled out an envelope with five pictures and showed them to the pilots.

"Were any of these people in the Ladas?"

Both pilots quickly pointed out Susan, Brian, and Walker.

"Got ya! Now I know they are all still here," the director said. "But where did they go?"

Both pilots said they were hit with a powerful weapon.

"Forensics will figure out the weapon type tomorrow.

I need to know if you recognized the fourth man from the two Ladas?"

The pilots shook their heads. "*Nyet!*"

The FSB director left and went back to his Baikonur office. He called his USAF WEBMAZE insider on her new burner phone.

"We verified your WEBMAZE team pictures. We know the team is still here, but we may have a sixth spy. Do you know who he is?"

She answered firmly, "No, but I know the teams usually have a native situational assistant that supports them while in-country."

"It's early there and I assume you are either at work or on your way to work. Dig into the team's status and find out who the local man is," the director ordered.

She snapped back, "Like I said before, I am read into all the WEBMAZE compartments, but I am no longer privy to the team's activities. All interactions with the team are now through General Black—who has been sequestered in his office for the last few days."

"The team must eventually surface somewhere—especially if they are trying to flee the country," the director said. "You need to be more aggressive; your mother is counting on you!"

FSB counterintelligence director Arkonov immediately called his best field agents to meet with him later that day. He still had no status for the agent he sent to the Sputnik hotel. The meeting was short and tense.

"The team of five American spies must be found. There may also be a local helping them. If they have not left the country, they will probably reappear near the cosmodrome again. Search all the nearby cities for any Americans that do not appear to fit in. Do not shoot to kill! We need to question them about their mission here. Work in teams so we do not have a repeat of the helicopter fiasco! Go!"

The case was starting to make him look inept and he needed a success under his belt. This American team was better than he was told and willing to take risks. The twin helicopter takedown was unimaginable to the FSB investigation team. The fact that they were both shot down with large caliber rifles was shocking.

The latest call, from the first deputy chief of the GRU, General Vladimir Alekseyev, had been very pointed and clear.

"Director Vasilly Arkonov, if you do not capture the Americans in the next few days, your career is over. Do you understand?"

At the crack of dawn, Rick woke Walker and Brian and explained what happened the previous night. "The Alligators were surveilling the highway all night! I suspect there'll be roadblocks looking for the two Ladas."

"Shit, we need to ditch the Ladas and get other vehicles." Walker pulled Vladimir aside. "Do you think Andre would agree to trade his old farm truck for two newer Ladas?"

"If he realizes he is coming out on top, of course."

"Then work the deal. We need his truck."

The Ospanovs were in the middle of preparing breakfast for the team when Vladimir approached Andre.

"I would like to discuss a trade with you."

"Vladimir," Andre said, "we can discuss business after breakfast. Irina and I have made baursaks with kaymak and sliced lamb sausage. We have tea as well."

After breakfast, Vladimir sat with Andre and opened the vehicle discussion.

"Andre, my American friends would like to travel on backroads, but the Ladas are not capable of driving over rough surfaces. I noticed the truck in the barn has large wheels and is high off the ground. The Americans are willing to trade you the two Ladas for the truck you have in your barn."

"Vladimir," Andre said calmly, "no one in their right mind would trade two Ladas for my old beat-up truck. My counteroffer is that I will only trade you for the Ladas if I can get my truck back when the Americans are through with it."

"Andre, you drive a hard bargain. You can keep one Lada, but the other must go back to the Americans when we bring the truck back. Do we have a deal?"

Andre thought for a moment. "Yes, we have a deal. But when do I get my truck back? I will need it in a few weeks to move hay into the horse barn."

Vladimir knew he was lying when he said, "The Americans will be leaving the country in a week. You will have it back by then."

Andre was pleased. "You have a deal."

Walker was pleased that Vladimir worked out the trade.

"So, why did you agree to return the truck?" Walker asked. "Wasn't the deal good enough as a trade?"

"I think Andre knew my story was phony when he said 'no one in their right mind would trade Ladas for my old beat-up truck,'" Vladimir said.

Walker knew Vladimir got out-traded again but was hoping the old couple would not call the police when they left.

"Did you get a sense that Andre was overly suspicious about us? I heard him ask if I was former military."

Vladimir was confident. "Neither Andre nor Irina were suspicious. They like Americans and were happy for the visit. When I agreed to return the truck, I knew Andre was only too happy to win the trade. Besides, he has my Rolex Submariner probably worth over thirteen thousand US dollars."

Andre gave the truck key to Vladimir, who handed it to Walker, who backed the truck partly into the barn. That way, neither of the Ospanovs would see the weapons. It took a few minutes to transfer all the equipment and weapons from the Ladas to the truck. Walker decided that he would drive the truck, which was more like an oversized Woody but with room for only two more up front. Susan and Vladimir sat on the bench seat. Brian, Jared and Rick piled into the back seat, which was torn and uncomfortable to sit on.

Rick joked, "Oh sure, the 'upper class' gets to sit on a real seat while us peasants get to brave the raw cushions and springs."

"Yeah, yeah, whatever," Walker said. "Just make sure the mags are full and the weapons are ready. We're still suspicious looking to the local police, who are probably all in on the search now. Brian, call ahead to the safe house and let them know we're coming in a truck. If they ask about the Ladas, tell them it's a long story—sort of like the two collided Alligators."

As they pulled into the driveway, Irina ran out and handed Vladimir some of her Bavarian crème charlottes along with a bottle of wine.

"*Do svidaniya,*" she said and waved goodbye along with Andre, who stood in the doorway.

The team was on M32 in a matter of minutes. With the possibility of being found and captured, the mood was tense. On the way to Dzhusaly, Walker thought better of his being the driver and pulled over, telling Vladimir to drive.

Their first encounter with a politsiya roadblock was uneventful, with all the occupants faking sleep. The police asked Vladimir where he was going. He answered in

Russian. "Dzhusaly on farm business." They let him pass through without waiting the few minutes to verify the truck registration or even checking the other passengers. After all, they were looking for two grey Ladas.

Rick and Jared gripped the MP-5s with their fingers next to the trigger. Walker said under his breath, "Bureaucracy is the same everywhere. These guys aren't serious about their business."

Vladimir defended them. "I suspect that the FSB did not tell them why they wanted the politsiya to look for us. That would have changed their attitude."

The second politsiya roadblock was a few miles outside Dzhusaly. This time Walker told Vladimir to detour around the blockade by taking some back roads that Walker recalled seeing on the Dzhusaly city map. They were neither followed nor did they arouse suspicion. Another good decision, just one of many that put Walker on Dr. Kit Green's list of military personnel with "supernormal genomics," or a keenly developed sixth sense. He had been scheduled by General Black to arrive at Dr. Green's lab in two months for DNA testing. Things had come a long way since the STAR GATE program days.

The ride got bumpy on an unpaved road that roughly paralleled M32 the last few miles into Dzhusaly. Unfortunately, the old truck had old tires and one just gave out. They piled out to see what happened and there it was— the front right tire was flat as a pancake. Rick and Jared looked for a spare and found it, alone with a jack and a lug nut wrench.

"Do you think we'll have to walk the rest of the way?" Susan asked Vladimir.

"Not unless the lug nuts are stuck!" Vladimir said.

"Call the safe house and tell them we'll be late," Walker told Brian, who immediately made the call.

"The safe house agents said there are multiple roadblocks and police all over the main city roads. The agents will be watching for the Ospanovs' truck on the way in," Brian said.

Rick and Jared replaced the tire and threw the hardware back into the truck. Then Rick yelled, "We're done—let's go."

With Vladimir at the wheel they continued their five-mile trek to the safe house. After another thirty minutes of a slow bumpy ride, they intersected M32 inside Dzhusaly and wound their way along the river to the safe house.

14

GENERAL BLACK WAS approached by the lead telemetry specialist, Robbie Chan, along with Richard Callahan, the WEBMAZE technical team leader.

"Sir, we correlated the U-2 data with the telemetry data and it appears there were emissions or signals coming from the satellite that were not communication signals. They were more representative of phased jamming or noise signals in the microwave region at a wavelength of 1.5 mm or about 200 GHz—the least absorptive frequency range in the atmosphere. The surveillance video is being analyzed by Lonnie Thompson, and we should have his analysis this afternoon."

"What did the U-2 pilot record that appears to be so odd?" General Black asked.

"The IR sensor recorded a bizarre series of heat spots on what looked like a matrix of small barges being towed by a trawler-sized boat. The boat itself was lit up in both the IR and radio spectrum."

"What radio frequencies were active?"

The analyst said, hesitantly, "Oddly, all the voice radio frequencies. And they were all sending a test message that repeated."

"All the frequencies?" questioned General Black.

"Yeah, I thought that was odd too, and the spectrum analyzer noted significant RF signal attenuation when the IR was strongest."

"I want your report by tomorrow night—even if it's incomplete," the general said, sending Lonnie on his way. This was a breakthrough, but General Black wanted more data before sharing any news with the SECDEF or the other WEBMAZE team leaders. He needed more to present the full situation to President Marr.

The next day, General Black, along with the WEBMAZE satellite signal experts, met in a TOP SECRET SCIF at the Pentagon.

"Okay, team, you have thirty minutes to explain what the hell that satellite is all about," General Black said.

The lead analyst, Richard Callahan, a thirty-two-year-old Cal Tech genius, explained, "Yes sir; the correlation between the satellite signals and the U-2's multispectral data analysis indicates a highly-focused, high-powered microwave beam with accurate ground targeting capability. Based on recent classified Russian technical papers, their scientists have made a few critical breakthroughs in the ability to focus a high-intensity microwave beam at 200 GHz as a potential terrestrial weapon system. There are two Russian weapon systems in development—the Ranets-E and Rosa-E. Both are short-range HPM defensive directed energy weapons designed to fry aircraft avionics and missile system microelectronics. However, it is entirely possible to put a similar HPM system into space, especially with an advanced power regeneration and storage system."

"So, how did the Russians get so far along with a space-based weapon system under our noses? Did we have a clue at all?" the general asked.

Callahan was at a loss, but Marsha DuBois, the lead analyst for space weapons technology from the National Air and Space Intelligence Center at Wright Patterson Air Force Base, piped up. "I think I can explain."

"Then speak up!" the general huffed.

"Well, sir, we have collected telemetry data on two other satellites in the last year that we originally thought were collecting signals but were actually radiating a pencil laser beam to targets on the ground. It took months to position a sensor field in the Russian Urals to determine the performance of the laser. Thanks to your field team, we learned their ability to target surface systems."

"So, how good are they?" the general asked.

"They can pinpoint a ground target within five feet— and that exceeds the necessary capability to be an effective space weapon. Although not officially classified as a weapon or threat, the Russians learned the targeting geometry and atmospheric corrections necessary to build an effective future space weapon system, which I now presume may already exist on board Cosmos 2455."

"I recall a report summarizing that capability over a year ago—with the conclusion that the Russians would take another seven to ten years to develop a space weapon," General Black said. "Well, now we're unfortunately playing catch-up and have to accelerate our plans. Only weapons of mass destruction are illegal in orbit according to the 'Outer Space Treaty' of 1967. Has the field team collected enough data to take control of this satellite?"

Robbie Chan, WEBMAZE telemetry specialist, spoke up. "Sir, the satellite telemetry signals are encrypted, and we will need more data to correlate maneuvers with control signals. The NSA already has the telemetry data stream and is attempting to crack the code. The U-2 pilot captured the weapon's operational configuration but not the corresponding control signals. In order to take control, we need to collect uplink commands and correlate them to satellite maneuvers. It may require multiple field collection teams over a few weeks, but the cosmodrome is the ground control site."

That was music to General Black's ears.

"Okay, team, get to work collecting everything we can about this bird! Let's all meet again tomorrow at 0800."

What General Black knew that no one else cleared for WEBMAZE knew was that the US already had three high-powered laser systems in low earth orbit on call with rules-of-engagement approval from POTUS. Only those cleared for HAVE BLUE under the DARPA TOP SECRET Excalibur program knew about the space weapons. The general feared that the Russians already knew about HAVE BLUE and planned to destroy all three laser weapon satellites. They were each launched with a cover story about gathering detailed earth surface elevations in support of the National Geospatial Intelligence Agency's, or NGA's, need for a more accurate digital terrain elevation database—or DTED for short.

General Black knew of two sanctioned laser-weapon firings; the first was at a Chinese satellite to destabilize it, and the second was at an old US weather satellite to deorbit it into the sea. Each satellite could employ its beam in a self-defense mode in case of a physical attack. Their operational range was limited to 150 miles, capable of space use only. This new Russian HPM DEW satellite posed a serious threat to any satellite through its ability to destroy electronics at a long range, for which there was no defense.

The WEBMAZE security staff was kept busy. The woman handling all the security clearances from the Hanscom AFB facility realized something big was going down. As soon as she had a break, she called the director of FSB counterintelligence and said, "You might be interested to know that there have been WEBMAZE groups converging at the Pentagon with attendees coming from all over the US. General Black was there as well, so command decisions were being made."

Director Arkonov asked, "So, how many are we talking about? Ten? Fifteen?"

"No, more like thirty people—all WEBMAZE cleared. That's more than at any time during my tenure as a guard here!"

"Okay, keep me informed of these meetings. This is a good thing to know—keep on it! Maybe you can find out why they are meeting. And get me the name of that sixth person! Has the lie detector testing begun?" asked the director.

"Yes. They have tested fifteen people already. My testing will be in a few days."

"Remember, just lie about everything," said the director. He hung up.

The woman felt that something really bad was about to happen—and she might be stuck in the middle of it.

15

THE TEAM WAS grateful to make it to the safe house at Dzhusaly. Vladimir had driven like an old lady so as not to arouse suspicion. The two agents, Howard and Nuro, were sure no one followed them down the streets to the driveway entrance.

"What would you have done if we were followed?" Susan asked.

"You don't want to know; let it go," Walker said.

"Well, actually, now that we've been discovered, I'd like to know what to do if we get caught."

"We went over this during mission prep," Walker said. "If we're captured, we simply surrender, and we all stick to the same story. We are here to purchase land as an investment for a hotel. We all have IDs that match that story."

"Do you think they'll torture us?" Susan pressed.

"We all took an anti-thiopental drug that makes your body resistant to truth serum. Torture is used only as a last resort."

That was a lie, but Susan needed answers, so Walker had no choice. He needed her to perform the mission should they get new orders. And he didn't want to get into the discussion about the reaction their bodies would have to thiopental, also known as sodium pentothal—an almost uncontrollable, continuous vomit reflex.

While the rest of the team had a late meal in the kitchen, Walker went into the SCIF room and dialed General Black.

"Steve! Glad you all got back to the safe house. We heard about the two Alligators going down and the search for your team. Did they see any of you?"

Walker was reluctant to admit that the team's identity was compromised. "Unfortunately, a drone spotted us as we were leaving and got replaced by two Ka-52s. The pilots must've seen us, but don't know if they actually had time to video us. I would assume they did. Did the home team analyze the telemetry data we sent?"

"Yes, but I can't elaborate at this time," General Black said. "A U-2 out of Kadena gathered live signals and IR/EO data that looked like high-powered microwaves as Cosmos 2455 passed over the Sea of Okhotsk"

"A weapon system? Jammer?" Walker guessed.

"It would seem. We need your team to execute additional missions in the next few days. Now that your team is compromised, I'd normally just end the mission— but there's much more at stake now. Is your team still ready to go?" General Black asked. "Do you think they can execute additional intercept missions?"

"Susan is tough, but she didn't expect things to go 'south' so badly. Vladimir's concern is that he was ID'd and could be disclosed as a CIA operative."

"We need your team to be effective or we'll have to replace it," General Black said sternly. "This mission just jumped ahead of every other priority mission in the DoD! Let me know by 0700 local whether your team is a go."

"Yes sir; 0700 it is."

Walker would have to do some fancy pep-talking for both Susan and Vladimir—and it needed to be now. Walker went into the kitchen with a big smile and said to the team, "General Black sends his congrats on a successful mission. He also said that our last data dump was highly valuable and is already producing critical information. Unfortunately, this mission just jumped to the number one priority for the USAF and DoD. Let's go into the SCIF."

Walker went into the SCIF with the rest of the team following. Rick was last in and closed the door.

"Initial analysis back home determined that Cosmos 2455 carries a high-powered microwave directed energy weapon system. The boss wants to know if we're all ready and able to perform a few more missions. Since it appears that our covers are blown, and our identities most likely compromised, everything's more complicated. So, is everyone on board?"

"I get that this is a priority mission, but can we really still execute it?" Susan asked.

"And I have been gone for way too long from the ranch and need to be there to task my ranch hands. I need to get back soon—like tomorrow," Vladimir added.

Walker, seeing that he was on the defensive with Susan and Vladimir, decided to get open support from his military guys—Brian, Jared, and Rick.

"Are you guys ready for more action?"

In unison, they said, "Sir, yes sir!"

"This op stands out as one of my best ever," Rick said. "Never thought I'd ever get to shoot down a helo! Can't believe it went down like a spinning sack of potatoes."

Jared agreed. "So far, we have done everything right— even escaped what looked like certain capture, twice. This is what I trained for."

"I really want to support the team, and I understand how important the mission is," Susan said. "But the risk of getting caught is getting awfully high."

Vladimir piled on. "Too many people have seen my face for me to just go back to my horse farm. If the FSB has my picture, I am a dead man."

"I understand the reluctance to take on such a huge risk, but we signed up for this because we all know how important the mission is," Walker said. "We can't just sit here and wait till things cool down. General Black needs our support now and we're the only ones in-country to get the job done."

Susan relented. "You're right. I took this job knowing I can use my expertise for special missions like these, but staying focused could be a problem."

"Seriously? You're great under pressure. Just think of this as the final few laps of a biathlon!" said Walker, who knew he had to go one step further. "Our other unofficial role is to protect the civilian teammates on these missions. We don't take that lightly."

"Right, boss," Rick said. "We took an oath to protect all civilians on these missions. We'll do whatever it takes."

"So, how many additional missions does General Black need?" Vladimir asked.

Walker pondered Vladimir's question in light of the new analysis by the WEBMAZE team. "We'll support as many missions as General Black requires. This satellite must be compromised. So, I ask again, are you in?" Walker asked Susan and Vladimir.

"Yes, of course," Susan said with a hint of indignation. "But since you mentioned biathlon, can I have a weapon too?"

"And, yes, I'm in too," piped Vladimir. "But I will need to check on my lead ranch hand to make sure all is well."

"Good. All in for tomorrow night!" Walker said. "Get some sleep. We might be out again in the next few days. Susan, if you still want a weapon tomorrow, I'll have Rick set you up with a Glock."

They left the SCIF and went to their designated rooms and crashed until daybreak.

16

GENERAL BLACK DECIDED to get the WEBMAZE tech team together to weigh a few options to present to Walker's intercept team. When the full team had assembled, General Black started.

"Listen up; the good news is that the AQUADUCT field team made it back to the safe house. We need to come up with ideas for a longer intercept simultaneous with a second U-2 pass over the Sea of Okhotsk." Looking at Robbie, Marsha, and Richard, he asked if anyone had ideas. "The clock is ticking."

"If the intercept team can get closer to the Sea of Okhotsk, we can correlate the satellite signals with the U-2's recording of the weapon system's actions," Robbie said.

"It would be unlikely the team could get to Okhotsk in the next day or so," Richard said. "It's over fifty-five hundred miles from Dzhusaly. What about outfitting a second U-2 for collecting the satellite's telemetry data? Is that possible?"

General Black recalled that Buzz had mentioned a few options the Dragon Lady could employ in addition to a spectrum analyzer. The one that would be ideal was a telemetry tracking and recording system. He excused himself from the meeting, saying, "Stick around. I think Richard may have something."

General Black immediately called Colonel Lighthart. "Buzz, can you task two U-2 platforms for an overnight collection over the Sea of Okhotsk? The mission just got real hot. We may be dealing with a new specialized weapon system. What d'ya say?"

Lighthart, whose pilot had just flown a U-2S mission over the Sea of Okhotsk, had operational concerns. "We may have lucked out on that pass over Okhotsk but may already have jeopardized my birds."

"Buzz, you know I'd never ask for two birds without a good reason—and this one tops the list. The last U-2 overflight yielded extremely valuable ELINT and signals analysis. We need the same support tonight but with an additional U-2 capable of collecting two-way satellite telemetry data in the 1670 MHz to 1710 MHz range with high-gain antennas on the top and bottom of the fuselage."

Buzz was reluctant to commit two of his four U-2Ss on a single mission knowing that the radar footprint for two birds was almost four times more likely to draw a threat response.

"Sir, before I commit the birds, is there intelligence indicating a minimal threat footprint?"

General Black, having operated in this climate many times before, knew that the Russians were careful not to attract attention to any specific geographical area by installing batteries of SAMs or transporter/erector/launcher systems, known as TELs.

"I can say with eighty-eight percent confidence there are no known threat systems surrounding the Sea of Okhotsk."

"Okay then, General. You will have two Dragon Ladies on the mission tonight. What time should they start their sweep?"

General Black scanned his cheat sheet. "According to our team, the next late-night pass over the central portion of the Okhotsk Sea will be 0130 Local. We will need your birds there thirty minutes before and after that time with the video, sensors, telemetry, and recorders rolling."

"Do you really want video of the sea surface as well?" Buzz asked.

General Black thought about it and joked, "If you can get video, audio, infrared, low light, radio fingerprints, and X-rays, I want it all."

"Well, sir, we can do all that except the audio. We're just up too high for that. The video will contain low light and infrared. Sorry, but we would need another two days for any other mission."

"Why two days? I always thought the mission subsystems were modular and easily interchangeable."

"Yes sir—modular," Buzz said. "But the thing about 'modular' is that not all modules can be flown simultaneously. The U-2S is a tiny aircraft—not a Boeing 707 like the E-3 AWACS."

Heading back to the WEBMAZE team, General Black hoped he was right about the ground threat. All his intel sources confirmed there were no local surface-to-air threats. All hell would break loose if a U-2S were shot down; and worse, the Cosmos 2455 science project would go silent. If the mission were successful, post analysis of the telemetry might allow the US to control the satellite. As General Black entered the secure Top Secret WEBMAZE conference room, he explained the situation.

"Colonel Lighthart agreed to fly a two-ship U-2 formation over the Sea of Okhotsk, one to capture the telemetry signals and the other to capture the satellite's HPM radiation and the effects on the victim ship. If anyone would like specific data or radiation collected, chime in now."

"Ask if the pilots can monitor and record the signals on their voice comm radios—in particular, VHF-AM, VHF-FM, UHF-AM, and HF USB," Robbie said.

"I hope they don't ramp up the power level too high while the U-2s are in the radiation field. The pilot could lose control," Marsha warned.

"Thanks for the info. Callahan, stay tuned!" General Black ordered. He immediately went to the STE in the outer office to call Buzz Lighthart back.

"Buzz, two things the team mentioned. First, have your pilots leave all their radios on, and if they can record their signals, do that too. And secondly, make sure the pilots can fly the plane manually through a mini-EMP because they might be flying through an HPM beam."

Buzz assured the general. "Sir, these guys can fly the U-2 with the engines shut off and no instruments. I will call you the minute they return."

"Buzz, I owe you one—a big one. A lot of pressure, I know, but this is a critical mission. Thanks for the support."

"Yes sir! I do like a challenge. I'll tell the mission systems crew and the pilots right away."

General Black next contacted his counterpart, General Henry "Hank" Johnson, the head of the Directed Energy Directorate, part of the Air Force Research Labs located at Kirtland AFB, New Mexico.

"Hey, Hank, long time no see. Last time we talked, you were on the brink of developing a new HPM device!"

"Hi, Joe," answered General Johnson. "It's been really busy here. Between development, test, and redesign, we are pretty close, but not ready for prime time. The Army has taken the lead on this now that the DoD plans to field the first HPM weapon on a truck—most likely an MRAP vehicle. It's your dime, so what's up?"

"Have you been staying on top of Russia's directed energy weapons program? We might have come across something you'd be interested in," said General Black

"Yeah, and now you've got my undivided attention!" said General Johnson.

"Based on recent signal intercept analysis, we think the newly launched Russian satellite, Cosmos 2455, may be sporting an HPM DEW."

"Seriously?" asked General Johnson. "We thought they were five to seven years away from a working terrestrial HPM DEW—but a space weapon? Not likely."

"Well," answered General Black, "then you're as surprised as me. Can you provide one of your experts to support our team? It's a high priority."

General Johnson was reluctant. "The tech leader is Dr. Alfred Michelson; he is wrapping up his support of a contract award to Verus Research—experts in the effects of high-powered electromagnetics on electronics. He should be done next week."

"That's too late for us; we need him yesterday. My guys are not read into your programs, so they don't appreciate DEW technology."

"Okay, Joe, I will have him at your Pentagon office by CoB tomorrow. How long will you need him?"

"Thanks for your support on this. We'll need him until we figure out what kind of DEW we are dealing with.

Besides, I'm sure Dr. Michelson will be excited to find out what the Russians are up to."

General Black next went to his office and called the WEBMAZE field team at the Dzhusaly safe house and asked for Walker.

"Center, this is Agent Howard. Who would you like to speak to?"

"Put Colonel Walker on," said the general.

"Sir, it's Steve. Any updates to the situation you can share?"

"Steve, I hope you and the team have recovered. There will be two U-2Ss flying signal intercept missions tonight over the SEA of Okhotsk and, according to the WEBMAZE techs, they could be in danger from high-powered microwaves. I will need your team to go back to the cosmodrome and get the satellite signals during the overpass but continue to track the satellite for as long as possible before losing contact. We need to collect enough to know what signals are sent before the testing over Okhotsk begins. Is your team up for this tasking?"

"Well, General, the team is ready to go, but I'm a bit worried about Susan. She was really shaken up over the last mission, although I think she's tougher than she thinks she is. My guys have guaranteed her safety—but she knows there are no guarantees."

"I can't emphasize enough the importance of this mission. I know the stress is great, but we really need the data."

"Sir, we'll have the whole team out there tonight. I'll let you know before we head out."

"Good luck to you and the team—we're counting on your success."

17

WALKER WOKE UP before the safe house agent's wake-up call. He needed to make sure that Susan was ready to execute the next mission and that a new vehicle could be found. Then there was the Vladimir complication. Vladimir needed to return to his horse ranch, but he was the team's expert on clandestine intercept locations around the cosmodrome. His knowledge of escape routes and Russian logic was critical. Going back to the cosmodrome without both Susan and Vladimir would be extremely risky and could result in mission failure—or worse. On the other hand, Susan's inability to maintain focus could become a liability for the team.

Walker got cleaned up and went into the kitchen where Susan was already making herself a ham-and-swiss sandwich on a baguette. Every morning around six, there was a delivery of fresh breads to the safe house as requested by the owner, who had agreed to set up the deliveries per contract. Susan was particularly fond of the baguettes, and when she got nervous, she ate.

Walker approached her and said, "That looks good. You mind if I make one?"

Susan was looking around for mustard when Walker handed it to her. "This what you're looking for?"

"Matter of fact, it is," answered Susan as she took a seat at the kitchen table. Walker followed.

"So, Mac. What was it that convinced you to join clandestine field ops?"

"It's complicated. Why do you ask?"

"For me, it's simple; as the team commander, I need to understand what makes people tick and what motivates them. Take Brian for example. He was getting bored in a nine-to-five communications system acquisition job at Langley and wanted to get more involved with actual fieldwork. It turns out he's one of the best field agents I've ever worked with. JD and Rick are trained in unique MOSs but are natural field operatives. They're fearless, quick thinking, and problem solvers. What I know about you came from your personnel file. I still don't know you or your personality. You probably already know it, but you're the most educated person on the team."

Susan smirked. "If I'm supposed to be so smart, then what the hell am I doing here? Henry, my neurosurgeon boyfriend, thinks I'm nuts for doing this stuff."

Walker knew about Henry from her file. "You agree with Henry? You obviously like pressure and working in a special ops environment."

Susan was impressed by the Army officer's intuitiveness. "Actually, you're partly correct. With the blonde hair and young-looking face, no one took me seriously at work. When a position for a CIA field operative with a PhD in orbital mechanics opened up, I applied. It wasn't until my first field operation that I realized how really important my expertise was—and the rush I experienced while executing a clandestine mission sealed the deal. I love this work, but I'm not so sure I want to put myself in life-or-death situations anymore. I plan to get married, settle down, and have kids—and I only have a few years left for that."

"We'll do whatever it takes to get you back, but there's always some risk in every mission. Remember what happened in Crimea? Not all missions go smoothly."

Susan recalled the unexpected bombing of their intercept position by Russian separatists; Walker got them all to safe territory. She knew that the team would be looking out for her welfare.

"In my discussion with General Black, he recognized your critical support on this mission. He coordinated with Colonel Lighthart the launch of two U-2S Dragon Ladies for an intercept mission over the Sea of Okhotsk; one will be intercepting the telemetry signals sent to and from the ship and the other one will be recording the HPM."

"Do you think this'll be our final mission so we can leave this godforsaken place?"

Walker made no promises. "The U-2s will gather telemetry signals during the satellite overpass. The WEBMAZE techies say it's the telemetry signals from the cosmodrome that initiate the satellite's weapon system."

"General Black needs us to execute another intercept mission tonight while the U-2s are flying over Okhotsk?" asked Susan.

"Yup. We're the DoD's best hope for neutralizing this threat. Based on feedback from the NSA, General Black believes there's a WEBMAZE mole tipping off the Russians about us. But the mole is locked out now that only a few key WEBMAZE staffers are in the loop. FSB may be looking for us, but they know nothing of our plans. So, Mac, you in?"

"Yeah, I'm in. Let's get this done."

"I can't promise this'll be our last mission, but I'll do everything in my power to get you back to the US of A alive and well. By the way, you still want a pistol?"

"Thanks, sir, but no. I'll trust you guys to do all the shooting."

Walker gathered up the team and explained the mission for tonight. Vladimir was visibly concerned.

"If things go badly and I can no longer return to my ranch, will the US honor my request for asylum?"

"The CIA rules on asylum allows for situations just like yours. I'm positive the US will accept your defection from Kazakhstan—if you choose to do so. We can discuss that further when we return." Looking at his team, he said, "Ready all weapons and mission equipment, and make sure all batteries are fully charged and ready to go by 2200."

Vladimir and Walker discussed alternate intercept locations and selected two relatively close together in case one was compromised. Tonight's mission would be difficult to execute due to the FSB's dogged resolve to catch the team.

"None of the selected intercept locations have natural or man-made cover for our operation," Vladimir said.

"Noted," said Walker.

18

THE FSB SECURITY detail had to cover the three most likely intercept locations. Director Arkonov requested the estimated times Cosmos 2455 would be overhead at night. *Surely the Americans would never consider a daytime mission,* he thought. *Or would they?*

"Gear up and get out to all the locations before dusk," the director ordered the three field teams. "Set up the motion and sound sensors, the perimeter monitoring system, the sniper's hide, and establish the drone routes. If you see anyone that even remotely appears to be the Americans, capture them and immediately contact me."

The director had tried earlier to call his WEBMAZE mole on her burner phone and got no answer. Unbeknownst to Director Arkonov, the mole, one Harriett Wilkings, decided to run. Even her local handler didn't know where she was.

Wilkings underestimated the FBI and was captured by agents in St. Louis. License plate cameras spotted her car and the FBI swooped in. They had been just hours away from giving her the lie detector exam to determine if she was the mole leaking classified information to the Russians.

The FBI dug into all the WEBMAZE team members' financial statuses. They learned Harriett had over $130,000 in a bank in the Caymans. The FBI also found out that her mother received a kidney transplant in Canada and somehow paid for a donor's kidney, the surgical transplant operation, all necessary medications, and the recovery expenses, totaling nearly $280,000. That far exceeded the income resources of a MTREC security guard with a typical salary of $77,000. There were no bank loans or equity loans of record. When Harriet's boss asked her to come back to work on her day off, with no explanation, she knew she was toast. They seized her burner phone before she could throw it away.

The FBI figured she might have tipped off her handler, who they now knew was the FSB director in charge of counterintelligence, Vasilly Arkonov, assigned to the security of all cosmodromes and other high security facilities. After checking her phone and the incoming and outgoing calls with the carrier, they knew she had not contacted her handler before fleeing—probably for fear of retribution. Harriet begged the FBI to protect her mother, who was still in recovery at a Canadian hospital.

Director Arkonov was concerned that his missing American mole had been captured by the FBI. If so, he would have her eliminated immediately. Next would be her mother. He still did not know the whereabouts of his best agent, could not find or capture the Americans, and worst of all, had lost two Ka-52 Alligators! *Can things get worse?* he wondered.

Six hours before their planned mission departure, Walker thought it would be wise to check out the two intercept sites that he and Vladimir had thought were best for the mission. He figured if the FSB had any intelligence at all, they would be waiting for them. So as not to unnecessarily spook the team, Walker quietly went to Brian.

"JD and I are scouting out the two sites proposed by Vladimir, as a safety precaution. If anything goes wrong, I'll send a distress signal via the satphone directly to the safe house. I already told Howard, but in the meantime, you're in charge," Walker said.

He then tapped JD's shoulder. "Without arousing suspicion, get our Glocks and MP-5s and ammo and meet me in the garage."

Walker's favorite sidearm was the Glock 21 Gen4 chambered in 45 ACP with thirteen-round mags. Unfortunately, its weight and larger bullet caliber did not fit with the mission.

Walker met Jared out in the garage. "Where we goin', boss?" Jared asked.

"We're gonna do a little reconnoitering before the mission. Are the binos in the car?"

"Of course, boss, never leave home without 'em. I also brought a few temblors and the NVGs just in case."

They picked one of the two dark-red 2015 Toyota Venzas; the safe house agents got great deals on them. The side and rear windows were tinted, and everything fit with room to spare. Walker got into the driver's seat while Jared finished loading. As he started the car, a GPS unit turned on and a map display appeared. Walker was impressed with the agents' foresight and tech savvy. Walker punched in the coordinates for the two locations and off they went.

An hour later, as they arrived at the first location, they noticed an unexpectedly large number of people at the site, a space-vehicle-themed recreation park south of the cosmodrome. Men were playing soccer on a makeshift field; children played kickball, and others were simply spectators—an awful lot of them. After watching for a few minutes, Walker saw that some of the spectators were wearing earpieces and talking, but not to anyone nearby. And they all had smartphones.

In the distance, Walker made out an SUV parked on a hill, facing the park. Two people were seated inside. Then he noticed people sitting in other vehicles parked nearby.

"JD, get the binoculars out and tell me what you see in the car up that hill."

"Boss, it looks like two men in uniform, and I think they're armed. It looks to me like a stakeout. Too many people not acting naturally."

"I think we better get out of here before we're spotted," Walker said. "Put on your Stormy Kromer hat to hide your face." Walker did the same.

"Boss, you look like a poor Cossack in that hat. Maybe we can do selfies with these hats later."

Walker was not surprised that the place was also selected by FSB. He hoped that the other site was not compromised. As he selected the second GPS location, he realized there were two ways to get there; one was the long way around the cosmodrome, and the other was a more direct route. Walker elected the long way around. Ten minutes into the drive, he noticed a few large black vans— SWAT-type trucks—coming their direction. As the Venza approached the second intercept site, Walker realized all the trucks and a few military vehicles were bivouacking approximately 800 yards from his team's next site.

"Shit, the FSB folks are getting real smart real fast," Walker said. "We can drive by them and continue up the road past the rear cosmodrome entrance. Try to get a picture of the trucks and APVs as we drive by."

Jared pulled out his cell phone. "Okay, boss! Got it."

Walker decided to check out at least one more place before going back. "JD, watch for any tails as we drive through the area."

"Boss, where the hell we goin'?"

"Since both of the first two sites are compromised, we've got to check out a third, a fourth and a fifth if necessary."

After driving for another twenty-five minutes, Jared yelled, "Holy shit, boss! This is the farmhouse where the Russians almost caught us on that first night!"

"Look around with the binos and check for any suspicious activity. We'll need to check the other sides of the building," Walker ordered. "We could use Vladimir's tunnel to get in there."

The abandoned farmhouse looked peaceful and inviting during the day—a really nice piece of property. *Too bad some farmer had to give up his farm for the space race*, Walker thought.

It was close to dusk but still light enough to see whether the Russians had left monitors in place. Walker was satisfied and drove around the farmhouse. Jared checked for booby traps and trip sensors.

"Boss, I see one of the temblors we planted on the first op. Stop and I'll get 'em."

Walker stopped the car and Jared jumped out. The Russian team that chased them over three days ago must have found no evidence of the American team having been there. *They screwed up again*, he thought.

"JD, get back in the car; we'll come back here tonight. Keep your eyes peeled for anything suspicious. When we hit M32, send a text message to Brian that we're on our way back."

Jared pulled out the encrypted satphone and sent the message to the safe house satphone.

Susan became curious about Walker and the sergeant's absence and asked Brian, "Where did Colonel Walker and JD go? They've been gone for quite a while now."

Brian remained calm. "Colonel Walker and Sergeant Stone decided to check out the intercept sites for security. Not to worry; they'll be back shortly."

About twenty minutes later, Walker and Jared nonchalantly strolled into the food pantry looking for something to eat. Both seemed upbeat but not very talkative.

"You two are grinning like the Cheshire cat from Alice in Wonderland," Susan said. "What's up with you, anyway?"

Walker thought about how to describe their reconnoiter activities without generating too much concern. Gesturing, he got them all together in the SCIF, then explained.

"When Vladimir and I settled on two new places to set up the op, I realized the FSB would probably do the same. So, JD and I decided to check 'em for security risks. Unfortunately, the FSB staked out the same two places, so we had to look for an alternative location. Remember the old abandoned farmhouse, the one with Vladimir's escape tunnel? Well, that place was not being watched—at least, neither of us could see any suspicious activity."

"Don't be so sure," Vladimir said. "They may have put motion sensor monitors around the building as a failsafe measure."

"Maybe, but I got out of the car to get the temblors that Rick and I put in the ground and no one showed up," Jared said.

"That doesn't mean anything," Vladimir said. "Maybe they only activate on command, or maybe after dark. As Sun Tzu said, 'Never underestimate your opponent.'"

"Vladimir is right," Walker piped. "We still need to be cautious going there tonight. We'll take the tunnel in to avoid being seen near the farmhouse."

"Don't forget, I armed the booby trap bomb when we went into the tunnel," Vladimir said. "It would have to be reset."

"What're you talking about?" Susan said, alarmed.

Vladimir forgot that only the military guys knew about the tunnel mine. "I thought the whole team knew!"

"Seriously—am I the only one that didn't know about the bomb?"

"In any case," Vladimir continued, "I will reset the booby trap since we may need to escape from the farmhouse again."

Walker was always thorough, but this time it really paid off. He made a promise to Susan. "We'll make sure you get home safe and sound." He didn't want to think what might have happened if the team had gone to either of their first two surveillance locations.

"Okay, people, do we have all our technical gear ready to go? Batteries fully charged? Guns and ammo? Protective gear? Headlights and flashlights? This may be our last opportunity to get the two-way signals for Cosmos 2455, so make it count. We head out in two hours—so get some rest and go light on food and especially drinks, starting now." They all left the STE room except Walker, who immediately contacted General Black.

"General, sir, we're ready for the mission tonight. Are there any last-minute changes, details, or direction?"

"We have good news and bad news; the good news is that we discovered the mole and she is spilling her guts. She was giving away your location, which is why the Russians were on your tail. The bad news is that her FSB handler now has names and pictures of each member of your team—except Vladimir. Unless he's compromised during this mission, he will never be suspected. And no— no mission changes from here. We do need the intercept, and remember, continue to collect until the signal from Cosmos 2455 is too weak to record—as far on the horizon as possible."

"Roger that, sir. So, who's the mole? Do you know everything she did to compromise the mission?"

"She was one of our security guards and had access to almost everything," General Black said. "The FBI is interrogating her now; we'll know more in the coming days. As far as she knows, there are no other moles. Of course, the Russians wouldn't have told her even if there were. I'll explain more when you get back. Good luck; we'll be waiting for the upload."

Walker wondered who the mole might be. He could recall six female security guards that worked the WEBMAZE vault. Walker's understanding of double agents' motivations centered on their need for recognition and money. Treason was almost never over ideology. He reluctantly decided to withhold the general's revelation from the team for the time being and went to bed for a nap with a request for a wake-up by the safe house agents around 2145.

19

THE LAST FEW days had been very successful, and the satellite was operating flawlessly. The unfurling mechanism for the array of radiating elements, the very high-power microwave amplifier, the onboard optical targeting system, the computer and software, and the datalink communication system all worked perfectly. The response time for retargeting was an acceptable three minutes, and the accuracy was well within half a barge's width—approximately twenty feet.

The Reshetnev Information Satellite Systems company typically designed and delivered GLONASS satellites for navigation and EKSPRESS communication satellites. But in early 2003, it was commissioned to develop Cosmos 2455. It was designed and built in a top secret building away from their main campus in the closed city of Zheleznogorsk, Krasnoyarsk Krai, near the city of Krasnoyarsk.

Even though hard times hit the aerospace industry in 1995, space interests were always a Russian government priority, especially for the military. Although control of Cosmos 2455 was primarily from the ground station at the

Baikonur Cosmodrome, it was possible to send emergency commands from two specially outfitted trawlers in the Southwestern Pacific and Northeastern Atlantic.

Cosmos 2455's HPM would be at half power during its pass over the barges. The *Yuriy Ivanov* SIGINT ship's microwave power sensors were calibrated for the test, which was expected to knock out the computer-controlled radios on the barges—except for the HF radio. They prepared the encrypted onboard satellite communication systems for the Iridium and Inmarsat to protect them during the pass. The scientists needed an efficient means to report back the effects of the HPM test in detail immediately after the test was over.

The U-2S Dragon Lady pilots were airborne and climbing to mission altitude—approximately 70,000 feet MSL. They coordinated their flight plans so as not to interfere with each other. They departed the Sea of Japan and headed north to the Sea of Okhotsk, flying over the location where they saw the barge matrix. Only four things could stop their mission now—aircraft or sensor problems, an abort-mission order, intruder aircraft, or missile threats. The special mission equipment was tested as operational just prior to departure from Yokota Air Base. They were all "GO."

The *Yuriy Ivanov* spy ship was almost in place. It was preparing to make a turn that would encompass a five-mile radius because of the sixteen interconnected barges. It was the ship's third thirty-day deployment in the past five months and the crew was worn down. After this test, a replacement crew was supposed to arrive.

The ship's captain hoped for a promotion and an award for his dedication to the dangerous mission. Pulling a string of barges took precision and enormous technical expertise.

The captain was selected because he was extremely efficient at performing complex boat maneuvers and maintaining an alert and technically proficient crew. He was also a steadfast Russian patriot, coming from a long line of Russian naval commanders. The time had come for his skills to be tested again.

The captain sounded the alarm and came on the PA system: "All crew members—prepare for the test. When the alarm sounds, everyone go belowdecks and shut all doors and hatches." He knew this pass could do real damage.

It's all coming together, he thought. *Mother Russia will finally get a huge advantage over the US in space.* With about twenty minutes before the satellite pass, he sounded the alarm and set the controls for remote operation belowdecks. After a quick walk around the decks to make sure everyone was accounted for, he quickly got belowdecks to the remote operations and communications room.

20

WALKER WAS AWAKENED by Nuro at 2145. He got dressed and made sure everyone else was up and moving. The team was fully assembled, equipment packed and ready, batteries charged, with weapons and ammo stacked. Out in the garage Walker told Rick to load the Venzas. Susan, Brian, and Vladimir were in Rick's Venza and Jared was with Walker. Five minutes later they were on the road.

Leaving the security of the Dzhusaly safe house was daunting for Susan, but she knew she was in good hands. This time they knew the farmhouse layout but had to enter via the escape tunnel. Walker had described his plans to scan the farmhouse first to make sure it was clear.

Arriving at the outer perimeter of the farmhouse grounds, Rick parked where they had parked on their last op. It was very dark, and they turned off their lights when they were within 800 yards of the poplar tree line. They waited for Walker and Jared to arrive before getting out. Walker slowly drove around the front of the farmhouse looking for any suspicious signs but didn't see any.

"Boss," Jared whispered, "it still looks deserted."

With dual-spectrum NVGs, any IR and low-light sources would be easily seen. But there were none. Walker whispered, "Let's hope there are no traps to warn our FSB friends."

Walker came full circle and met the rest of the team at the tree line. They all got out, grabbed their gear, and headed toward the storage shed. Before they left, Jared planted a temblor sensor near the cars and set the frequency to his smartphone receiver.

Although she was in the middle of the pack, Susan's heart pounded as her adrenaline kicked in. Walker and Vladimir led the way down into the tunnel where Vladimir took the lead and, upon reaching the farmhouse, defused the booby-trap bomb. As Vladimir was about to lift the floor trapdoor, Walker said as quietly as possible, "Wait! Before you lift the door, let's check for wires or sensors."

Walker slowly lifted the trapdoor and checked for any wires. He took out a small mirror to see if there was anything unusual on or near the trapdoor. "Clear!" Walker lifted the trapdoor high enough to get access to the room—then went up and in. "All clear—ready for setup!"

"Sir, we should do a quick scan for any bugs or sensors." Brian asked.

"Do it quickly!"

Brian got out the NSA-issue micro bug-finder and scanned the room, including walls, ceiling, and floor. Finding nothing, he whispered, "No bugs!" Jared and Rick quickly set up additional perimeter sensors at the farmhouse entrance and put their NVGs on.

It was about an hour before the expected pass of Cosmos 2455, and all their equipment was already up and running. Susan settled in—after all, she was the best in the business, she reminded herself—but her heart was still pounding.

Walker performed an Iridium satphone radio check just in case everything turned to shit. It was twenty minutes to signal capture and things were going smoothly until Brian yelled, "There's another satellite signal coming up on the receiver processor!"

Susan checked her laptop for nearby satellites.

"It's a Chinese communications satellite on a slightly higher frequency. It's in a higher orbit with less signal power. You might have to filter it out with the dynamic active filter. It will be crossing over Cosmos 2455 during our collection."

Brian quickly set a notch filter to null out the Chinese satellite's signal. "Done. The interferer signal level dropped 45 dbm. We should be okay now."

Just as Brian finished talking, Susan saw that Cosmos 2455 would be breaking over the horizon. Susan called out, "Five minutes until visible—initial radial 246.5 degrees, elevation ten degrees."

Brian set up the antenna in the direction Susan had called out and engaged the auto-tracking software that read Susan's laptop. Susan called out, "Record now!" Brian set the signal intercept computer into track mode and the recording started. As before, the signal started fairly weak but started to build in strength. The antenna-tracking algorithm worked like a charm and kept the antenna right on the center of the satellite's main beam.

About twenty minutes into the op, Walker thought he heard a hum outside.

"Douse all lights!" He whispered to Jared, "JD, check what that humming sound is."

Jared quietly walked to one of the broken windows out front and scanned with his NVGs. At first, he didn't see anything—then he spotted it.

"It's a small six-prop drone with a video camera underneath moving sideways in a semi-circle around the front of the farmhouse."

"Shit! They probably saw the Venzas and got suspicious," Walker said. "They didn't bother to guard this place because they're using drone bots for surveillance. If they don't see anything unusual, maybe it will move on. How much longer, Brian?"

Susan answered for Brian. "The satellite goes over the visible horizon in ten minutes."

"Mac's correct—ten minutes," Brian said.

Walker now knew why there were no people watching the abandoned farmhouse. The Russians were taking advantage of the latest innovations in drone technology.

"We didn't see drones this afternoon, so I guess we underestimated the Russians," Walker said.

"We've got to destroy it or distract it," Jared replied. "I could shoot it down, but that might raise suspicion."

"What if we could disable it—say, shoot at only the camera? Are either you or Rick that good?"

"I'm in a pistol league and shoot with a Model 41 at bullseye targets much smaller than that camera!" Rick said. "I'm sure the MP-5 can do it. With the red dot optics, I can put a round through an egg at a hundred yards. As long as it's hovering slowly, I should be able to take it out."

"Okay, take the shot, but avoid being seen by the drone! We don't have much time left. Brian needs to complete the collection!"

"I'll set up where it seems to loiter longest and slowest— the front of the farmhouse," Rick said. "JD, let me know if a second drone shows up so I have time to duck."

Rick watched for the drone. He set the selector to single fire and slinked out the broken front door and set up his MP-5, using the porch rail as a gun rest. He heard the buzzing sound and saw the drone hover off to his right and, against the dark night, saw the camera system hanging from the center. He lined up the shot and pulled the trigger. Nothing. He must have inadvertently switched the selector to safety when he snuck onto the porch. Rick muttered under his breath, "Shit!"

As he quickly clicked the selector back to single from safety, the drone flew toward him. He ducked behind the porch rail and waited for it to move away, but it didn't. It hovered, staring at the farmhouse door for what seemed like an eternity, but then finally flew back and hovered, giving Rick an even better shot.

There was a muffled poof and the camera blew into pieces. A second later the drone flew up a few feet due to the unexpected weight reduction and then settled back to the preprogrammed hover height. The drone hovered in the same place for about two minutes, then it just rose up and zipped off in the direction of the cosmodrome.

"Nice shot!" Walker said. "Wait there for the replacement to show up! If it does, we may need an encore performance!"

"Like shooting the balls off a hawk!" Rick said.

Not five minutes later, Jared yelled out, "The replacement bot is here!"

"Everyone get down—cover anything that emits light!" Walker ordered. "There's another bot out front! Rick, can you take this one out too?"

Rick watched intently as the drone maneuvered over the area where the first drone's video camera hit the ground. It appeared to be surveilling where the camera pieces had fallen.

"Rick, what's goin' on?" Walker asked.

"Boss, I think it's surveilling the broken camera, and if it sends back video, they might figure out what happened."

"Shoot it down," Walker barked. "We can't let it return or send video!"

"Yes sir—it's a goner!" Rick set the fire selector to three-round bursts, and less than five seconds later the MP-5 ripped the camera and the drone to shreds.

"We've got about ten minutes before an armed recon team arrives. Let's move. Gather your stuff and get ready to jump into the tunnel on my call! Rick, JD—watch the perimeter for intruders. Susan, is the satellite over the horizon?"

21

THE U-2S PILOTS had already started their sensor monitoring over the barges' last known position. They went radio silent and had their radios in receive-only mode with their recorders running. The optical scan of the barges in the various light spectrums was getting really weird looking—lighting up one barge at a time like a twinkling Christmas tree until all sixteen barges had been lit up.

Both U-2S pilots knew what latitude and longitude to avoid during their pass, having pre-programmed the Cosmos 2455 satellite track into their flight plans. They understood an HPM could easily take out their avionics. The data recording continued well beyond the end of the lighted-barge phase, for another fifteen minutes. They collected a treasure trove of ELINT data, including the strange video recorded on the IR optical sensor.

Walker wanted to end the data collection. "Have the signals dropped off yet? It's time to go!"

"According to the satellite track, it is now nearing the five-degree horizon point," Susan said.

"Signals stopped! Shutting down!" Brian said.

"Good," said Jared, who spotted a drone recovery team fast approaching the farmhouse. "They're here and in force!"

"Pack it up and get into the tunnel—NOW!" Walker ordered.

"They're within two hundred yards and closing!" Rick called out.

Brian packed up the intercept suite, Susan packed up her laptop and modified iPad, and Vladimir opened the trapdoor and yelled, "Into the tunnel!"

Susan went in first, followed by Brian, then Vladimir, Jared, Rick, and then Walker, who pulled closed the trapdoor and attached rug over it. After Vladimir reset the booby trap, they all walked in the dark through Vladimir's tunnel for a second time.

At the end of the tunnel, before anyone went up into the field storage shed, Jared said, "I just got a temblor sensor alert by the vehicles—I think there's a waiting party by the Venzas."

"Use the NVGs to check out the landscape," Walker said.

Rick whispered, "Roger that, boss. JD, I'll go first—cover me."

Jared whispered back, "Right behind you." Rick and Jared both put on their NVGs and Rick slowly opened the shed door. Bad news. He saw three guards standing around the two Venzas—heavily armed with armor and comm gear integrated into their suit. He looked back at the old farmhouse and saw multiple flashlights all over the place.

Rick pulled the door closed. "Three guards, heavily armed, no NVGs, farmhouse is crawling with threats, but

Venzas look okay." Walker was not too surprised by Rick's heads-up. "We've got to get to the Venzas and report back ASAP."

Looking at Rick and Jared, Walker said, "Take the guards out! We'll wait for your signal."

Just as Rick and Jared stepped out the doorway, there was an explosion and a huge flash, and then a blast of air from the tunnel almost blew the rest of the team out the door.

Vladimir yelled, "The tunnel mine!"

Rick and Jared dropped to the ground and watched the three guards run toward the farmhouse. As soon as the guards were out of sight, Rick yelled, "The guards are gone—run to the cars—NOW! Follow me!"

As the rest of the team ran to the cars, Jared covered them from the storage shed. They split up between the Venzas, Walker driving the first and Rick driving the second. The cars were not disabled. Jared, the rear guard, jumped into Walker's Venza and they took off.

The U-2S pilots returned to base with a treasure trove of data plus some weird and unusual pilot reports. They landed without incident, and even before the jets came to a stop, their data payloads were being dumped. In the next twenty minutes, all the data collected was sent over encrypted SIPRNet via Inmarsat satellites.

It was ten hours later at the Pentagon, late morning, when the WEBMAZE team was ready to start analyzing the data. General Black was on the STE with Buzz and thanked him for the rapid response from his U-2S surveillance team.

"Buzz, the data your guys collected is being crunched as we speak. It all looks good; thanks for your support on such short notice."

"Sir, these guys live for this stuff! They would live at the edge of space every day! Anytime!"

"I'll let you know what this is all about someday over beers," General Black said.

Director Arkonov was in a rage because of the farmhouse fiasco.

"Don't you idiots do anything right? When the drone came back with the camera blown off, why didn't you send a special recon team right away? Now we have five people dead and nothing to show for it except two broken drones. Who was guarding the vehicles?"

The three soldiers guarding the Venzas put their hands up.

"You three—get over here! Will you be able to find the two Venzas?"

The senior guard answered, "Yes, Director. We also have their registration plates."

"Then start hunting for them! Now!" For the first time, the director realized his job was truly in jeopardy.

The captain of the *Yuriy Ivanov* SIGINT ship was getting satellite comm from the cosmodrome.

"Captain, was the test successful?"

The captain was eager to relay the good news.

"Every barge was radiated in the designated sequence and every radio except the HF radios were totally destroyed. There were no negative effects to the ship. The calibrations from the last test pass were perfect, and you will be getting the full report by tomorrow night before we dock."

"Captain, upon arrival, please report to the colonel for a complete debrief."

The captain wondered why the debrief was expected so soon after docking. Everything went perfectly—maybe too perfectly.

22

THE WEBMAZE TEAM was setting up the post-processing for all the U-2S data collected over the Sea of Okhotsk when General Black walked in.

"Where are we with the U-2 data? Has the field team sent back their data? Is the data readable and valid? When can I expect the initial eval?"

"Sir, we've been working on the data from the moment it arrived," said team leader Richard Callahan. "A quick check of the data finds that there was a very high-powered microwave test fired from Cosmos 2455 at all sixteen barges in a tight pattern. It also appears that test electronics on each barge literally blew out with the HPM radiation levels."

"Excellent! What else?"

"Dr. Michelson determined that there were multiple voice radios communicating across the spectrum—HF, VHF, UHF, and SHF on each barge—and that they all stopped operating, except the HF radios. As for the field team, no, they have not sent their intercept data yet."

"Callahan, good debrief! All this data and analysis will be labeled Top Secret AQUADUCT SI/TK SAR. Let me know when the field team data arrives. I want this satellite to be ours," the general said.

The field team, on the run again, was in search of an intercept-free location. Instead of going southeast to Dzhusaly, Walker decided to head north and west on M32 toward Ayteke. Near the northwestern edge of Baikonur, Walker pulled over and waved Rick alongside.

"We're goin' to the nearest parking lot and getting rid of the Venzas. Follow me." Walker found a large parking lot near a hotel and drove in. Rick pulled alongside again.

"Let's park the Venzas over there," Walker said, pointing to an area next to some trees. "Rick, JD, find two different vehicles, jump-start them, and pick us up. We'll be waiting by the Venzas."

"We're on it," Rick said. Rick and Jared split up and wandered over to some older vehicles parked out of direct view. Probably worker vehicles.

Susan was still thinking about what happened to the soldiers when the booby trap exploded in the tunnel. "How many soldiers do you think we killed? You still think we're getting out of Kazakhstan?" she asked Walker.

"Absolutely! We've been at least one step ahead of the FSB all along. The tunnel mine saved our lives—and kept our mission from failing. We're in a location that no one would suspect. We'll head northwest to Ayteke, look for a deserted side road along the way, drive far enough to guarantee no monitoring, then upload the data."

Looking at Vladimir, Walker asked, "You seem awfully calm. What's up?"

"Well, now I am, as you Americans say, toast. The FSB will be relentless in finding the owner of that farmhouse and tunnel. My life here is over. I can never go back to my horse ranch."

"No one can tie that property to you," Susan said. "Maybe they haven't been able to ID you yet. And you might not have been seen by the helicopter pilots long enough for a positive ID."

Walker reassured him. "If you really feel that your cover is blown, we'll get you out of Kazakhstan and to the country of your choice. But before you decide, you should call the ranch and talk to your head ranch hand. Maybe nothing to worry about."

Just then, Rick drove up with a rust-colored Lada Vesta sedan, and a minute later, Jared drove up with a green Toyota RAV4. Walker assigned cars. "Brian, Vladimir, get in the Lada. Mac, get in the RAV4 with me. Let's go—Rick, follow us." They threw all their stuff into the back, jumped in, and soon they were back on M32 headed to Ayteke.

A few minutes out, Walker told Jared to take a side road, and a few moments later the two vehicles arrived at an abandoned maintenance yard. "Pull onto the dirt road next to that abandoned construction vehicle."

Jared stopped near the heavily rusted dirt mover, with Rick right behind them.

"Brian, set up here for the upload," Walker said. "We need to get this intercept to HQ now." Brian jumped out of the Lada with his data intercept computer and satcom datalink radio and miniature antenna, set it up in a few minutes, found the satellite, initiated the encryption, and started the upload. Brian announced, "Uploading has begun." Rick and Jared instinctively set up a defensive perimeter using the rusted vehicles as cover. While Brian was busy setting up and uploading the data, the rest of the team broke out water bottles and power bars and took bio breaks.

Brian noted that the upload had just finished and was successful.

"Okay, shut it down and pack it up." Walker pulled out the satphone, pressed General Black's speed-dial number, and waited for the encryption indication.

"We were expecting your call. All data was received and is being processed—right now. If you can, head back to the safe house—lie low. I'll call you tomorrow."

"Roger that, sir," Walker said. "I'll explain what happened here as well. Talk to you tomorrow."

As soon as Walker shut down the satphone, he ordered the team to the safe house. They all piled into the cars and drove to Dzhusaly on M32. It seemed like an eternity in the darkness of night but was only two hours. Susan rode silently, hoping this would be her last mission.

Walker thought it odd that there were no longer roadblocks or vehicle stops along the route—especially through Baikonur. But then, they were looking for two Toyota Venzas.

On their approach to the safe house, Walker noticed two GAZ armored vehicles parked at the crossroad to the safe house entrance—lights on. They weren't there before, so he decided to avoid them by turning down the street ahead of them. He waved to Rick to follow him. They drove up the street and encountered a third GAZ vehicle and drove past it, looking for any clues that there might be an unexpected welcoming party.

Walker decided to call the safe house to see if they had been compromised. He pulled over near a store a few blocks away from the safe house and made the call. The satphone rang with no response. That was a bad sign. Despite the satphone emission risk, he called the WEBMAZE headquarters.

"This is field team lead ID five, zero, three, Golf, Whiskey, Xray, seven, one; please connect me with General Black."

On the other end, the operator acknowledged, "Yes sir, please hold." A few seconds later, General Black answered.

"Steve, are you and the team okay? Why didn't you call on the safe house satcom?"

"Sir, we're all okay. We're in Dzhusaly just outside the safe house. The agents are not answering and there are three GAZ vehicles nearby."

"I'll cross-check. Are you in a place where I can call you back?"

"Yeah, but we can't stay here long. Out."

"HQ out."

A few minutes later, Walker's satphone rang. It was General Black. "The safe house is compromised."

Walker hoped the agents destroyed everything.

"Go to the safe house in Aralsk. The address and local number can be accessed on the satphone by your ID. Your data has been a critical piece for cracking the Cosmos 2455 control codes. Good luck, Steve. HQ out."

Walker clicked off the satphone. "We've got to get the hell out of here—NOW! The safe house is compromised."

Both cars immediately headed to M32 again. Once on the open road, Walker waved Rick over. "General Black wants the team to know that the data we just sent was crucial. He thinks the WEBMAZE team may crack the telemetry code because of it. We're heading to a safe house in Aralsk. Follow me."

Susan, always looking ahead and already worried enough about the compromised safe house, asked, "Does that mean we're done here? How far is it to the next safe house? And does anyone know if that safe house is okay?"

"Maybe. Over three hours. Don't know for sure." Walker yelled out to Rick and his riders, "Get as comfortable as possible—we've got quite a ride ahead of us." Walker turned to Jared, handing him the satphone. "Punch in my ID, look for Aralsk, then tell me the ETA."

23

WITH CONSENT AND approval from the upper echelons of the Russian government, the cosmodrome scientists decided it was time for a real-life test of their new weapon system—without compromising its existence. After the last test in the Sea of Okhotsk, Cosmos 2455 was slowly maneuvered easterly in orbit over fifteen hours. From the Pacific Ocean, Cosmos 2455 rose on the horizon over Baja and crossed the US diagonally from southwest to northeast. The command to unfurl the four HPM active phased array antennas having been sent, the satellite expanded in size with the four antennas adding to the focal power of the central beam. As it streaked over the US toward Canada, the exact ground target coordinates were uploaded via satellite relay—the Rainbow Bridge Toll Gate on the US side of Niagara Falls.

On the Canadian side, a specially trained Russian agent, hidden from view, waited with a pair of multispectral recording binoculars and a parabolic microphone designed to record both normal and infrared video and audio. At exactly eight in the morning, Cosmos 2455 fired a single three-second burst of coherent, high-powered microwaves at the toll gate on the Rainbow Bridge. There were multiple bright flashes, and all the lights over and around the tollbooth burned out simultaneously along with the electronics of one truck and two cars at the toll bridge.

A commotion formed at the tollbooth; people got out of their cars to see why the vehicles at the tollbooth weren't moving. Several people were complaining about their cell phones, yelling "My cell phone is dead!" Two tollbooth operators asked if anyone had a functioning cell phone.

From the Russian agent's perspective, it would appear to the authorities that a lightning bolt struck the area at the tollbooth and disabled the electronics there. *It may be months before anyone suspects a man-made EMP,* he thought as he drove away.

At the first internet café, the agent uploaded the encrypted video and audio he had recorded during the tollbooth strike. His assigned follow-up action would include monitoring the local and national news for any public details about the event. Did the tollbooths fail? What vehicle electronics were affected? Were all cell phones affected? What was the approximate "damage" radius? If it was lightning, was there a loud thunderclap? Any burned structure? What did personal interviews discover?

The Niagara Falls city police arrived at the scene and checked for injuries. Seeing none, they moved the three vehicles out of the way of traffic and controlled the traffic flow entering the tollbooth. The New York State Police came a few minutes later and started investigating the event. However, the Russians were not aware that these unexplainable events were automatically reported to the FBI, which subsequently dispatched a special investigative team to the site. After all, terrorism could take many forms.

The cosmodrome scientists deemed the results of the test successful and were already preparing for the next test.

A few more randomly selected civilian locations around the world would prove the value of the system before testing more difficult, protected targets—including military bases and systems. The Russians knew the US overhead assets could not monitor the status of Cosmos 2455 when passing over New York, so they would not sense whether the satellite had unfurled the four high-power phased array arms. And the laser ground station was too far east to see the satellite.

24

WHEN PERSONNEL FROM the special investigative FBI unit, the Science and Technology Branch, or STB, arrived on scene at Rainbow Bridge, they initially considered it a simple lightning strike. But after a few hours they got the sense that their lightning theory was not going to fit. There was no storm or even clouds in the area when the bridge lit up. So that left only one other option—an EMP device.

The STB unit had been trained to look for signs of employment of a high-power electromagnetic pulse device: low-voltage electronics in a small area were burned out, radios didn't work, and cars were dead. The FBI had even employed a mobile weapon called the EMP gun to stop federal criminals. Everything eventually pointed to an EMP device—but they had no idea where it was fired from, who could have fired it, or what type of device it was. The FBI collected the burned-out cell phones and any other small electronics they could find and sent them to the special analysis headquarters for in-depth evaluation.

The analysts looked over the remains of cell phones, GPS receivers, a few cameras, iPads, iPods, and four laptops. They all had failed processor chips, and all the receiver front ends were literally burned up—including cell phones, WiFi, Bluetooth, and GPS. However, not all the circuits were burned out. This led them to believe it was a high-powered-microwave-type electromagnetic weapon, but with a fairly tight beam. The FBI lead investigator determined the results of the analysis should immediately be marked SECRET/NOFORN because of the possibility that this was a terrorist attack. The STB unit collected all the local video camera recordings, and the analysts noted that the surviving video cameras caught the spatial aspect of the event; they realized the power density was centered over the bridge toll structure and weakened as it went outside the center. That could only mean that the HPM EM device was either on the bridge or above it. Fortunately, the results of the STB special report would be shared with all DoD, CIA, and other classified information users. Unfortunately, it would be twenty-four hours later.

General Black's WEBMAZE analysts were called to the conference room. The general pressed the team.

"So, are we ready to take control of Cosmos 2455 or what?"

"Sir, we have determined the codes for the HPM antenna control, firing signal, and targeting laser," said the team leader, Callahan. "We are still working on the orbit maneuver commands and, in particular, the deorbit command."

Robbie Chan, the signals analyst, said, "NSA has broken the existing encryption code, but there is no guarantee we can control the satellite yet. We're working with L2Cnet's datalink division to build a signal generator for fielding on either a Gulfstream 650 or 550 and get a beam-steering antenna installed as well. We have access to either aircraft type—seating for a max of fifteen and a flight range just over 7,000 miles."

"Okay, so how long before all that comes together in a functioning, mission-capable system?" General Black asked.

"Sir, we just got the call from the L2Cnet program manager," Callahan replied. "He said he can guarantee system fielding in about three months."

"What? We already have similar systems fielded and operational!" the general said, agitated. "Can't one of them be converted for our use?"

"Sir, we explored two other alternatives, and only one would deliver a functioning capability if converted," Callahan said, "but unfortunately at the expense of the existing program it serves."

"Okay, Callahan, what's the timeline for repurposing that other system?"

"Based on prior work of a similar nature, I would say six weeks, ready for testing."

"This is a priority program. We'll have to sacrifice the other program for now," General Black barked. "Is there any way to shorten the six weeks?"

"We can accelerate the equipment removal faster as long as we don't have to worry about its disposition," Callahan said. "Plus, the aircraft must be transferred to the L2Cnet facility in Texas by tomorrow night. That cuts out another week. The L2Cnet PM wants assurances that his team will get premium labor rates to get the work done 24/7 until completed."

"Callahan, whatever they want or need, make sure it happens. I want that system operational in a few days—not weeks—fully tested and ready to go. I also want status reports twice a day."

After the general stepped out, Robbie and Marsha stated their concern with the schedule, especially since the transmitter signal requirements were not finalized.

"Richard," Robbie said, showing some frustration, "what the general wants is not possible—we just figured out the required signal formats a few hours ago!"

"I agree with Robbie," said Marsha nervously. "What happens to us when we don't have a fully fielded system on his schedule?"

"Guys!" Callahan interjected. "We've done this before and in less time. What are the real problems? If it's manpower, we can get it."

Robbie explained, "The L2Cnet team expects detailed technical requirements for the datalink transceiver, like power output, signal format including pulse rates and widths, antenna gain and polarization, receiver sensitivity, and lots more, none of which is in ready-to-share form. And to complicate matters, we need to communicate with L2Cnet over SIPRNet or STE technical details that are TOP SECRET, with special access code words. This can only be approved by the Under Secretary of Defense Sheffield."

Callahan threw down the gauntlet. "You all heard General Black. He made this program a priority! So, unless we break any laws, any roadblocks to success will be dispatched immediately. If there's any way to execute this faster, tell me now."

25

LIEUTENANT COLONEL WALKER drove with Jared and Susan in the RAV4, and Rick was with Vladimir and Brian in the Lada. M32 at 0230 local was dark and desolate except when driving through Baikonur. On their way to the Aralsk safe house, Walker couldn't help but wonder what became of Howard and Nuro—the two Dzhusaly safe house agents. He hoped they escaped and destroyed anything that could link Walker's team to the next safe house.

Walker asked Jared to check in every thirty minutes to verify the status of the safe house at Aralsk with HQ.

"Center, this is field agent ID seven, eight, Quebec, Romeo, Tango, niner, zero—checking in."

"Sergeant—status unchanged from last. On schedule?"

"Center, we are on schedule. Out."

"Center, out."

Another thirty minutes passed without incident, but a few miles beyond the Baikonur exit, there was bright light ahead on the road. Walker immediate thought roadblock and pulled over. Rick pulled over right behind him.

Walker said to Jared, "JD, make sure the weapons are ready to go, just in case." Walker jumped out and ran back to Rick's window.

"What's up, boss?"

"There's a bright light up ahead and it looks like a roadblock or a checkpoint. We're looking for a detour. Brian, are there any detours around that area?" Walker asked.

Brian yanked an iPad out of his mini duffel bag and quickly scanned the area on the map. "Sir, this is the only mapped road between here and Aralsk. There might be side roads that take us way offtrack that might avoid the roadblock."

Walker's instinct was to evade the roadblock at any cost. "Okay, are there any rivers, valleys, mountains, train tracks, or other obstacles on the map?"

Brian pointed to what appeared to be a small river, maybe a creek. "The only thing I see is a creek that appears very small about thirty miles ahead on the south side of M32. It might be very shallow since we're in the dry season of Kazakhstan this time of year. The north side is too close to the cosmodrome to risk driving."

"We're goin' off-roading. Follow us!" Walker said.

Rick yelled out the window, "Roger that, boss. Just remember we're in the city car."

He ran back to the RAV4 and jumped in. "We're gonna drive offset south of M32 for the next fifteen to twenty miles or so and then get back on M32."

They took the first small road headed south off M32 and drove about three miles. Periodically smaller unpaved roads appeared on either side, so Walker decided to turn west onto one of the roads. At night, it was difficult to see the road ahead, but there were small farm-like buildings on both sides, almost all with the lights out. The smells of cow manure and cut hay wafted into the vehicles.

After driving cautiously over the rutted road with high beams lazing, Walker saw some lights headed toward his crew. He motioned for the two vehicles to pull over. When they came to a stop, Walker jumped out and ran back to Rick's Lada.

"I think we've got company," he said. "We're pulling over at the next farmhouse and setting up a defensive position. Follow me—and do what I do. Headlights off."

Walker ran back to the RAV4, jumped in, and said, "JD, if you see a farm, that's where we'll pull over."

"Farm on the right—one hundred yards," said Jared. Walker pulled up to the crude driveway on the right. There were no lights anywhere, but there was a small barn set off from the main farm. Walker shut off the RAV4 parking lights as he started into the driveway with Rick close behind. With no lights, Walker carefully maneuvered the RAV4 to the rear of the barn where there was a tractor parked nearby. Rick pulled in behind. Neither car was visible from the road.

Walker called out, "Mac, Brian, and Vladimir, get into the barn and take cover." Pointing to Rick and Jared he said, "Set up a defensive position on both sides of the barn. Bring the NVGs, sensors, guns and ammo. We can't take any chances."

Walker wondered if he should call the Center or wait until the situation was known. But there was no time; the lights were coming down the road Walker's team had just been on. He had to wait.

"If we get into a shooting match, take out their comms first," Walker whispered. "We can deal with the threat as it approaches. Don't fire until I say so."

A minute later a single GAZ rolled down the road. The blockade commander just happened to notice the high beams off in the distance and these soldiers were told to check it out. They noticed the lights disappear somewhere in this area and were told to pursue. Two of them had NVGs with infrared and were scanning the area. They noticed a heat signature of two vehicles turning into the driveway they just passed. So they backed up, and then partially entered the driveway. The heat trail led up the driveway, so they decided to disembark and search on foot. There were four soldiers, and none stayed in the GAZ.

Walker, Rick, and Jared watched all this from the hides they set up at the bottom edges of the sides of the barn. They also had NVGs with infrared. Walker knew if the soldiers came any closer, his team would all be seen and captured. As the four soldiers approached, they split up and pulled out their AK-74s; two went to the left of the barn and the other two took the right side. Hoping to find that the owners there simply had late-night business, they did not expect a real threat—to their detriment.

When they were halfway to the back of the barn, Walker yelled, "FIRE!"

Rick and Jared each let loose two three-round bursts from their MP-5s, and all four soldiers were down in three seconds. They never got off a shot. There was almost no sound as the suppressor technology did its job.

"Let's get the hell out of here!" Walker yelled. Brian and Vladimir ran back to the Lada where Rick had already dumped his weapons and ammo in the back and was waiting in the driver's seat. Susan ran to the RAV4 and jumped into the back seat. Jared grabbed his weapon and ammo and threw it in the back of the RAV4, then jumped behind the wheel. Walker quickly searched the four men for a radio and, not seeing any, yelled, "Brian, look for radios in the GAZ. They might be useful. You have one minute."

Brian saw only a small handheld radio. He grabbed it, ran back and handed the radio to Walker and ran back to the Lada. As soon as Brian got into the Lada, they fled. The lights came on at the farmhouse just as they exited the driveway, and they saw someone opening the front door. Walker realized they might have only a few hours lead—at best.

"JD, keep the lights off until the farmhouse is out of sight."

Rick did the same.

They were driving on some of the worst roads in Kazakhstan to avoid the roadblock. Susan realized that the hunt for them was getting more intense and awfully close.

"Would someone please remove the GPS trackers from these damn cars," she huffed.

"It's just good detective work," Walker said. "Few people here drive this late, so we looked suspicious."

"You might be right, but we've had too many close calls to call it good detective work," said Susan. "Maybe the mole knows our moves."

"I doubt the mole has any knowledge of our whereabouts or plans," Walker said. "I wanted to tell you all this when we got back to the safe house, but the FBI has caught the mole . . . Shhhh!" Walker was listening to a radio conversation in Russian; a commander was trying to establish contact with the four men in the GAZ. The commander repeated his request for a status report. Walker knew that the lack of response would set off alarms and a larger force would be searching for them within minutes. He hoped that the occupants of the farmhouse didn't have a cell phone or telephone, giving them a few extra minutes to escape. They just kept driving—slowly—with the lights off.

Another ten miles down the road, the roadblock lights almost gone, Walker told Jared to pull over at the next road headed north. Rick pulled over behind him. Walker got out, walked to the Lada, and checked with Brian.

"Does the map show this road north?"

"Unfortunately, none of these roads are on the map," said Brian.

"Yeah, figures. Let's take this road north to M32 anyway. Objections?"

"Sir," said Brian, "this road may go north, but there's no guarantee it goes all the way to M32."

"Got it, but we're heading north. Rick, follow us!"

They continued until they arrived at a small berm at the edge of M32 that was too high for the Lada to drive over. The vehicles stopped and Walker approached Rick.

"Your Lada will not get over the berm. It's too low to the ground."

"Boss, have you ever done off-roading? Trust me, this is a piece of cake. Give me a few minutes."

Rick walked over the berm and checked out what was on the other side. "Boss, the berm isn't the problem; it's the creek on the other side. I'll see if there's a shallow and narrower crossing farther up."

Rick found a narrow area of the creek a hundred feet further up, then walked into it to see if the creek bottom was too soft. It was shallow and firm—the perfect place to cross the berm.

"Boss, I found the perfect place to drive over, right there!" Rick pointed to his makeshift marker—a stick with a white handkerchief on top.

"Okay, we'll both cross there."

Rick said to Brian and Vladimir. "You guys are dead weight. Get out and walk to the other side in case things get crazy."

"Okay, boss, here goes." Rick started his roll along the berm until he was near his marker—then gunned it, hitting the berm at an angle. He rolled over the top, back down the other side and flew through the creek. He stopped on the shoulder of the eastbound side of M32, got out, and called to Walker.

"Made it! I'm on the shoulder of M32." Walker said, "Tricky maneuver. Okay, JD, you're up." Jared easily drove the four-wheel-drive RAV4 over the berm and pulled alongside the Lada. "Piece of cake!"

"Mount up—we're already late arrivals."

Walker called the Center on the satphone. "Center, this is Agent five, zero, three, Golf, Whiskey, Xray, seven, one. Status?"

"LtC Walker, this is Center—status unchanged. Sierra Hotel is still a go. Out."

"Agent out."

Walker thought the worst was behind them, and unless they hit another snag, they should be in Aralsk by 0600. Walker heard calls to the GAZ soldiers over the radiophone for almost forty-five minutes after the takedown, but the radio went silent after that.

Driving into Aralsk was not at all like Dzhusaly or Baikonur. The village of Aralsk was very rural and not nearly as developed as Baikonur. Its population declined severely in the 1960s when the Aral Sea was irrigated into oblivion upstream. The Aral seascape was littered with landlocked fishing ships since the seabed had dried up.

They were to drive to the Hotel Altair near the railroad station, then drive south to the pharmacy. Across the street from the pharmacy was the safe house. They arrived at 0615, almost on time. The building was fenced in and there was only one vehicle entrance. Jared drove up to the entrance and Rick followed.

At the entrance there was a vehicle gate, a door gate, and two small cameras. Walker yelled out so that Rick's occupants could hear, "Everyone, look into the camera!" An armed man came from a small guard shack about forty feet up the drive. He opened the door gate, came to

Walker's door and said, in a Kazakhstan dialect of English, "We have been expecting you and your team for some time. Welcome to Aralsk."

The guard then radioed back to the safe house and the vehicle gate opened. He then said, loud enough for both Jared and Rick to hear, "Drive all the way to the back of the property, then park inside the blue carport."

They drove to the blue carport, which was surrounded by a seven-foot-high wall. They parked, got out, and noticed that there was only one path leading to the rear of the house. It was almost dawn and they could see that the yard was bordered by beautiful flowering bushes. Another agent, a tall, slender man about thirty-five years old, came to the cars.

"My name is Alexey. You already met Bekzat. Askhat is inside monitoring the area. We are the agents in charge. All your equipment will be taken care of."

"No. JD, Brian, and Mac will walk back with you to the cars. They will get their equipment," Walker said. "The weapons and ammo can be moved by your guys. Thanks."

They walked with Alexey to the back door and were greeted by Askhat. They entered a huge foyer with plants all along the walls. "Where is the STE room?" Walker asked. "I need to make a private call."

"Follow me; it's just around the corner."

Walker dialed General Black's STE and waited for the crypto signal to go high.

"Steve, it seems you and your team got into a bit of trouble last night, eh?"

"Sir, there was a roadblock along M32 and we had to go all the way around it over back roads. Are Howard and Nuro okay?"

The general hesitated. "Unfortunately, no. They're most likely captured along with whatever remnants of classified data they couldn't completely destroy. They were never read into WEBMAZE, so they can't compromise your mission. They didn't know about the Aralsk safe house, so you're okay for now. We intercepted a report that four soldiers were killed last night. Was that you?"

"Someone at the roadblock must've spotted our lights. Then a GAZ with four men showed up in pursuit. They were closing on our makeshift defensive position; we had to take them out."

"Roger that. You did the right thing. I'll get back to you later today. You and your team need to get food and sleep to be ready for the next mission. I'll brief you on the status of Cosmos 2455 at that time. Out."

"Yes sir. Out." Walker thought, *Next mission?*

The FSB director was informed about the takedown of the GAZ and the four soldiers.

"I warned you about the American spies—they are very resourceful and dangerous. Did anyone see which way they were heading? Were there any witnesses to the shootout?" The conversation ended abruptly when the first deputy chief of the GRU, General Vladimir Alekseyev, called on another line.

"Director Arkonov, this is General Alekseyev. I was told that four of our men were killed in an ambush this morning. What is the status of the American spies?"

"They escaped again right after the shootout. We are questioning the owners at the farm about what happened there. We are also questioning the two agents we captured at the Dzhusaly safe house, but they are not talking. They may not know much more than who they work for. We are going through all the materials collected there as well. I have already ordered a deeper look at other villages for unusual activity. We are looking for a rust-colored Lada

Vesta sedan and a green Toyota RAV4 that were stolen from a parking lot yesterday. I am sure someone has seen them together somewhere!"

"You are running out of time, Director. If you need assistance of any kind, let me know and I will provide it. Just get the American spies! Oh, and congratulations are in order for the takedown of the CIA safe house in Dzhusaly."

26

THE LAST COSMOS 2455 HPM attack at Niagara Falls went exactly as planned. The agent's uploaded video showed surprising accuracy since the target was the US side of the bridge, specifically the tollbooth. Now it was time to attack a more complex target such as an airport or seaport—or maybe a large building in a large city. After discussing the ramifications of the next test, those in charge decided that the next target should be the Petronas Twin Towers in Kuala Lumpur, Malaysia. It was also decided that a night attack would be best for monitoring the effects. The concern was that this event might not get the same "emergency" response from the local police, who might suspect a freak lightning strike or odd power surge. Assuming successful satellite repositioning, the Russians would strike at eight the next evening.

Four Russian special agents would be required: two posted inside and two posted outside each tower to collect the data. Since the two inside would need to take video after the event, the video system would need to be in an

HPM-protected case. The two outside agents would video the scenario just prior to the event.

The satellite's orbit would need only minor adjustments to pass over Kuala Lumpur, and the adjustment commands were being sent only during the Baikonur passes. The Russian special agents would board aircraft that afternoon.

That night, the USAF command center tracking Cosmos 2455 noted a slight easterly shift in the orbit. Without the corresponding command telemetry, the WEBMAZE engineering team could not correlate the satellite's responses to commands from the Baikonur Cosmodrome. They needed more data.

Everyone settled in at the safe house except Susan and Vladimir.

"If we get caught, won't we all be shot as spies—in public?" Susan asked.

"Probably not. First, we're in an unknown safe house and the Russians don't know about it. Second, even if we're captured, we'd most likely be traded for a Russian spy—in a swap," said Walker.

"Are you serious? We shot down two helicopters, blew up a farmhouse, and probably killed ten soldiers; I doubt that they would ever let us go!"

"The FSB will be upset over our activities, but they will use you in trade to get their own spies back," Vladimir said. "In my case, unfortunately, I will most likely be shot as a traitor."

"I expect to hear from General Black in the morning. We'll know then if he needs additional SIGINT."

Minutes later, General Black called.

"General, I wasn't expecting to hear from you so soon!"

"Unfortunately, we just got informed that Cosmos 2455 slightly changed its orbit. We suspect that the Russians are planning to perform a test outside of the Sea of Okhotsk, but we have no idea where. In order to correlate the satellite's orbital responses to telemetry commands, we'll need your team to do an op today. Your team up for that?"

"General, if I may be frank, between the Dzhusaly safe house compromise and the Gaz attack last night, our team is exhausted. I know that Rick, JD, and Brian are always a go, but Susan and Vladimir may not be."

"Can you perform the mission without Susan?"

"That's a possibility, but I'll ask her. She'll have to program in the new orbit, otherwise we'll never see it coming."

"The Russians have ninety-minute intervals to send orbital change commands to Cosmos 2455, and they've just begun. Captain Mathers must collect telemetry data for at least two full passes to get the correlation data we believe controls the orbits. Can you do it? Your team may have to operate in the daylight."

"Sir, let me talk with Susan to see if she's ready. I will call you right back. Out."

Walker quickly gathered everyone together in the STE room at the safe house and started to explain.

"There's no sugarcoating this, so here goes. The boss just called and said Cosmos 2455's orbit is changing. Unless we provide the data that correlates the telemetry with the orbital changes, the opportunity to control this satellite is lost. He's also aware of our all-nighter to get here. If Mac programs in the new orbit, JD or Rick can assist Brian with the satellite and telemetry tracking. Mac, you and Vladimir can stay here and wait. Brian, can you do both the signals acquisition and the satellite tracking?"

"It's possible, boss, although that's a tall order in a short timeline. If Mac programs in the new orbit and then shows me how to run the software, I think—"

Susan jumped in. "Not so fast. It's not just programming in the new orbit. There are other settings that must be made. I'll need to talk with the USAF satellite tracking folks to get the data. Otherwise, yes, I think it can be done rather quickly, maybe in ten to fifteen minutes. Brian has enough to keep him busy on these missions. What made you think I wouldn't go?"

"I thought you were in overload from last night's craziness," Walker said. "I figured you'd want to sit this one out."

"To misquote Mark Twain, 'Rumors of my demise have been greatly exaggerated!'"

"Okay then, hop on the STE and contact your orbital SMEs right now. We need to leave here in the next hour. Brian, get your telemetry SIGINT gear charged up and ready to go. Rick, JD, get your intruder sensor gear, load up all the weapons, get extra ammo, and charge all the batteries. As soon as you're ready, let me know."

Walker knew he needed new transportation, so he asked the safe house agents for a truck that would blend into the local background. "Maybe a food delivery truck or a construction vehicle?" he suggested.

Alexey, the safe house "captain" said, "Yes, of course; we have a construction vehicle, a large van labeled *Pacific Ocean Bridge Building Company*. It's one of the companies the Kremlin uses to build and maintain cosmodromes. They are building the Vostochny Cosmodrome in eastern Russia. It is supposed to replace Baikonur's cosmodrome for most space launches sometime in 2019."

Walker was slightly embarrassed he hadn't thought of that cover earlier. "That's perfect! When can you get it fueled up and ready to go?"

Alexey was confused. "Do you mean you need it right now?"

"Yes, in the next thirty minutes! Can you do it?"

"It is located in our remote garage a few miles away. I think it is already fueled up, but it will take at least forty minutes to get it here."

"Why are you still standing there? Go!"

Walker went to the STE room and dialed in General Black's personal STE. "General, we're a go! Susan's on the other STE talking with your orbital SMEs—and she's going with us. We'll be out the gate in the next forty minutes."

"Glad to hear your team can support this tasking. It'll make a huge difference whether or not we can do anything about this satellite," General Black said. "I'll be waiting for your status report later today. Center out."

Alexey drove into the compound with a UAZ-3909 four-seater van. He stopped near the blue carport and jumped out. Walker's team was packed and ready. Before leaving, Walker said to Vladimir, "We won't need you on this run. We're setting up in a field with the van as cover. Call your peeps to let them know you're okay."

Walker hopped into the driver's seat, Brian rode shotgun, and Susan and Rick got into the back seats.

"Where's my seat?" Jared asked.

"In the back—get strapped in," said Walker.

They headed off to the Baikonur Cosmodrome, yet again. Jared broke the silence when they were almost on M32. "This thing isn't half bad. It rides like a jeep but feels like a Volkswagen bus!"

"Actually, it rides pretty good for a Russian van," Rick said. "And it has four-wheel drive!" he said, pointing to the second lever on the console.

It was an hour's ride to Baikonur and another twenty minutes to the cosmodrome. No roadblocks in sight. Susan decided to get ahead of the situation and pulled out her laptop. She watched the satellite's orbit.

"Cosmos 2455 is about fifteen minutes from breaking the horizon."

Brian checked his map app and said, "There's a large field north of here just seventeen hundred yards from the drome, well within intercept range of the side-lobe beam. Take your next left across the highway."

Walker crossed the M32 westbound lane and drove onto a dirt side road, putting the van into four-wheel-drive.

"We don't have much time," Brian said. "I suggest we go off-road and get as close as you can without being spotted."

"Brian, get all your gear ready to set up quickly. Rick, help Brian set up the antennas. Then you and JD set a defensive perimeter."

As they veered into the open field, Walker asked, "How's the equipment holding up?"

"The equipment is just fine," Jared said. "On the other hand, I'll need medical attention."

It got pretty bad for the next few minutes with the van bouncing around until Walker decided to stop. They could only see the top of the cosmodrome, but they were in the middle of a field in plain sight. This was close enough. Rick grabbed the uplink antenna and pointed it at the cosmodrome.

Brian set up the intercept receiver and the satellite tracking antenna and started the search, while Susan called out the pointing azimuth: "Cosmos 2455 is on the horizon at 228 degrees." Once the signal was acquired, the satellite tracking software kept the antenna on the satellite and within the satellite's signal beam. Walker, Rick, and Jared set up a defensive perimeter. It was broad daylight and they had nowhere to hide. They could see out almost two miles without binoculars.

Brian called, "Satellite signal captured," and a few minutes later, "Cosmodrome signal captured."

After about twelve minutes, Brian whispered, "Pass one intercept complete." Silence for the next ninety minutes was broken only by periodic train whistles and aircraft approaching Krayniy Airport. Everything went like clockwork. No one spotted their van for either of the two satellite passes—nearly two hours. Amazingly, both intercepts went off without a hitch.

The five now-exhausted special operators drove back to the Aralsk safe house, Jared at the wheel and Rick in the back. Upon arrival, Walker told Brian to upload both passes of data via the safe house STE. JD and Rick removed all the weapons and ammo from the truck and locked them down.

"Mac—it was a pleasure, as always!" Walker said. "Another job well done."

Walker called General Black. "Sir, we were operating in broad daylight, but no one noticed us. We had the perfect cover—a cosmodrome repair vehicle! Brian is uploading all the telemetry data from both passes as we speak."

"Thank your team; they went the extra mile today. Our people are already processing Brian's upload. Things can go to shit in a heartbeat—sometimes luck is on our side. I'll call you in the morning and let you know where we are. The orbital changes seem to have stopped. 2455 is in the new orbit. Center out."

A few hours later, the satellite control team at Baikonur had fully adjusted the orbit to pass over the Petronas Twin Towers in Kuala Lumpur that evening. At 1950 local, the four agents at the towers got into position. Agent One was inside Tower One on the forty-first floor at one end of the Skybridge and Agent Two was on the forty-first floor of Tower Two at the other end of the Skybridge. Agents Three and Four were outside, on opposite sides of the towers, ready to capture video of the building. A few minutes later, the towers were targeted; the lights on the upper floors flashed on and off for a few seconds like a Morse code signal, then went out. The lights on the lower floors flickered but remained on. To Agents Three and Four, it appeared as though a lightning bolt had hit the buildings. They saw many people in the tower lobbies waving their cell phones in the air and complaining that they were dead. Other people were overheard complaining about dead TVs, laptops, and tablets. The lobby desk supervisor eventually called the local police, who arrived about ten minutes later to investigate.

Inside, Agents One and Two pulled their digital video cameras out of EMP-safe containers and recorded everything. It was pure mayhem. People poured out of stores and businesses yelling for help. Emergency lights in some rooms seemed to work, but they were incandescent and powered by batteries. Only hotel guests with incandescent flashlights could light their way; all LED flashlights were burned out.

Agent One and Two's videos showed a very successful HPM attack, but Agent Three and Four's videos indicated that the attack seemed not to penetrate the bottom thirty floors.

After about forty-five minutes of post-EMP video, all four agents met outside as prearranged. Agent Three monitored the news media for any after-action notices in the news or on the internet. The news reported an unusual electromagnetic storm, which, for some odd reason, did not affect the bottom floors of either tower. The police were baffled and even scientists were not able to explain what happened. The event was all over the international news.

27

GENERAL BLACK ADDRESSED the collective group.

"Okay, team, what's the status? Did the telemetry correlate with the satellite motion? Did we learn anything else about 2455?"

WEBMAZE team leader Callahan spoke first. "Three things, sir. First, we have correlated the telemetry signals with satellite motion—and Robbie can fill in the details on that. Second, NSA has cracked the telemetry encryption. And third, we believe the Russians already tested the weapon over Kuala Lumpur last night. Marsha can provide more detail on that."

"Holy shit! The Russians actually tested their space weapon in the open? That's insane! Okay, Marsha, fill in the details."

"Well, sir, on CNN we saw that there was a report of a strange electromagnetic storm that hit the Petronas Towers in Kuala Lumpur, and that all electronic devices in the top fifty floors of both towers failed. We cross-checked the overhead pass of Cosmos 2455 with the outage, and they correlated—exactly to the minute the satellite was overhead. Coincidence? We don't think so. We believe that the Russians tested their HPM weapon system on Cosmos 2455 against the Petronas Towers."

"Great work!" said General Black. "Get as much technical information about the event as possible. Also, check to see if there were any other recent unexplained electromagnetic events worldwide, particularly below the orbit of the satellite."

The team leader, Callahan, spoke. "Sir, we were already searching for unexplained electromagnetic events and found one from a few days ago—at Niagara Falls. And yes, 2455 was overhead at the time of the event."

"The Russians are brazen testing their space weapon in the open, especially against US territory," General Black said as he pounded the table. "I need to know—can we program one of our existing satellite control systems to maneuver this satellite? I recall you and your team were working with L2Cnet in an attempt to accelerate conversion of an existing system for use on a Gulfstream—antennas and all. What's the status on that, anyway?"

"General, our L2Cnet team has already started conversion of an existing system and is waiting for us to provide details of the telemetry signal specifics like frequencies, pulse width, power output, antenna beam steering, antenna gain, and the encryption codex for the transmit function," Callahan said.

"Good info, Callahan, but I still need a date for going operational. Once L2Cnet has all the data you noted, how long before we can perform a mission?"

"Sir, they said the fastest they can be ready is seven days. They need to perform at least three ground tests and three flight tests before they can declare the system operational."

"That seems awfully formal, Callahan. Can they skip some steps and not affect safety-of-flight?"

"Sir, I will find out what steps they can skip and still meet safety-of-flight performance."

"Good—get right on that. I'm meeting with the head of WEBMAZE, Under Secretary of Defense Sheffield, the secretary of the Air Force, secretary of defense, and the National Security Council for a back-fill. We'll meet here tomorrow at 0730. Oh, before I go, does the field team need additional collection tasking?"

"No. Robbie and Marsha have agreed, the data collected is good enough—for now," Callahan said.

"Great work, team! I will let them know."

"Doctor Michelson at the AFRL Directed Energy Directorate has been in the loop on all our analysis," Callahan added. "He is, quite frankly, shocked and disturbed by the turn of events. Somehow their breakthroughs came faster than he expected."

Walker's STE phone rang.

"Steve, thanks to the data you and your team sent, the orbital maneuver code was broken. Hard to believe, but the Russians foolishly employed the HPM weapon system for testing. We're hoping to control 2455 in about seven days. You'll be glad to hear that the WEBMAZE SMEs say your SIGINT collection is done. Whenever you and your team are ready, get to the exfil safe house. We'll do whatever it takes to extract your team. Once again, your team came through!"

"Sir, I'll tell the team the good news. I'll admit, we had some close calls this op, and we'll all be glad to leave. Susan will be especially pleased."

"Are you bringing Vladimir in?" General Black asked.

"I'll leave that up to him," said Walker.

"Just make sure he's okay leaving his old life behind," said the general. "We'll have a hard time replacing him."

"Sir, that thought also came to mind. He's been a loyal partner for many years. I'll let you know before we move to the next safe house. Out."

Walker addressed the team while they ate lunch in the kitchen. "Good news! We can exfil Kazakhstan!"

Susan let loose with a "hallelujah!" Then, looking at Vladimir, Walker said, "General Black said if you choose to defect, you should come with us."

"Colonel Walker, I know going back could be dangerous for me, but I don't want to leave my farm. I appreciate the offer, but all I really need is a good reason for where I have been for almost a week."

"I'll respect your decision, whatever it is, but your life may be in jeopardy."

"I understand the risks," answered Vladimir, "but all I really need is, how you Americans say it, an alibi. I was seen by too many FSB people to have a simple one."

"What if you were to show up at FSB headquarters beaten and bruised claiming that a bunch of Americans held you hostage all week?" Susan said. "That might work."

"Yeah—I think it might," Walker said.

Just then Alexey yelled, "Intruders! Three GAZ troop vehicles slowly driving down the street and they are looking for something."

"Everyone, quickly and quietly grab your equipment and get ready to jump into the secret tunnel," Walker said. "Alexey, show my team where the tunnel is; I assume you know what to do if they attack the safe house!"

"This has never happened in the eight years we have operated the safe house," Alexey said nervously. "We will follow defensive and destruction procedures as directed."

"Bekzat, send out a Threat Level 3 message over the emergency Iridium channel," Askhat ordered. "Gather up all the crypto gear and satellite radios. Bring them to the tunnel."

Askhat watched the video feeds from the street cams and said, "The GAZ teams are off-loading and they appear to be splitting up and forming teams on each side of the street. They may not know yet that we are a safe house. One of them is holding an odd-looking antenna."

When the safe house was first purchased, all the cameras and the satellite antennas were installed with care so as not to be seen or identified by the public. However, that did not guarantee that transmissions could not be intercepted.

Askhat got a bit more alarmed when he saw four soldiers enter the backyard area outside the walls. Unfortunately, the RAV4 and the Lada were parked in plain sight.

"There are four soldiers coming into the rear of the property and they are moving slowly toward the wall. Two of them are scaling the wall—guns first. I think we are compromised!"

The eight Russian soldiers walking down the street stopped, spread out, and headed toward the safe house.

"Colonel Walker, get your team down into the tunnel," Alexey said. "The FSB will never find it. It leads across the street to the *apteka*—what you call pharmacy." Behind a kitchen pantry, the shelving rotated so that a person could fit through. Behind that was a secret chamber leading to a ladder down into the tunnel.

Brian and Susan gathered their equipment and went through the opening. Vladimir was third in line. Rick and Jared grabbed their MP-5s, pistols, temblor sensors, and ammo, leaving behind the two M107A1 50 cals and ammo. They were right behind Vladimir.

Walker said to Alexey and his team, "Follow the destruction protocol! We owe you guys. Best of luck."

As Walker walked hunchback into the hidden tunnel, he heard an explosion. The safe house had been breached; he knew Askhat, Alexey, and Bekzat might not survive. Their families would be compensated for their service.

Rick planted one temblor about fifty feet into the tunnel. A few minutes later, Brian popped up into a small room in the pharmacy across the street.

"Holy crap. This place is really small. We're stuck here unless we find transportation."

Susan and then Vladimir popped up next, both showing signs of panic. "Now what the hell do we do? We're trapped in a building they'll probably check!" she said.

Rick and Jared popped up next with all the weapons. "Did you drop a temblor back there?" asked Jared, looking at Rick.

"Yup, thought we'd need a little insurance."

Walker popped up last and said, "Heads-up, team— everyone okay?"

"So, how screwed are we? We have no safe house, no transportation, and no way out!" Susan said.

"The tunnel gave us time," Walker said. "We need to wait until night to find transportation and escape. Rick, did I overhear that you dropped a temblor in the tunnel?"

"Yeah, boss. I figured that would give us a little warning in case they find the tunnel."

Walker was not surprised.

"Should we plant some explosives in the tunnel to slow them down?" Rick asked Walker.

"No, that would only make us more vulnerable."

"So, if they find the tunnel, we just let them find us?" asked Jared.

"If they're coming through the tunnel, they'll know we went to the pharmacy, so we need to make it look like we escaped into the countryside," Walker said. "JD, see if there's an attic or basement with an area we can all hide in. If they find the tunnel, they'll come straight to the pharmacy."

Jared looked for an outside door and found one in back. There was also a stairway to a second-level storage area—but there was nowhere to hide. He left through the door to find another building they could hide in. There was a business a few buildings over with boarded windows. He ran to it and checked it out. The rear door was open and no one was around. It looked like an abandoned flower shop—and now an alternative hiding spot. The building was much bigger than the pharmacy and had three floors. He saw smoke coming out of the safe house and that a few of its front windows were blown out.

"There's an abandoned flower shop two buildings over," Jared reported to Walker. "The door was open and it has three floors and maybe a basement."

"Good job, JD! Everyone, get your stuff ready and we'll all head over to the abandoned building. Follow JD. Rick, you and I need to wait here until—"

"Holy crap, the temblor! Someone's in the tunnel already!" yelled Rick.

"Everyone to the other building—now! Move!"

The FSB director welcomed the good news from his field team commander, Major Pavel Golubkin.

"Director, we have found the other safe house and the two vehicles you were looking for. Your idea of searching for an Inmarsat or Iridium radio transmission was successful. Only one building in Aralsk was transmitting on Inmarsat channels."

Director Arkonov said, "I knew they had to be transmitting their status from another safe house! Not too many other villages for them to find safe haven. So, did you capture them?"

"Unfortunately, they escaped through a tunnel before we could. We are searching the area—and with six of them on the run, we should find them pretty quickly."

"Did the safe house agents talk?" asked the director.

"No sir. They are saying they did not know their names, why they were here, or where they went. But we did convince them to tell us about the tunnel."

"Commander Golubkin, keep the search going until you find them. We cannot afford to lose them again! Bring the safe house agents to me right away!"

The director got off the radio and immediately called for two aerial surveillance teams to watch over Aralsk. He thought, *The noose is tightening and I will finally catch the American spies.* He knew that he would lose his job unless he caught them all.

General Black was told about the Threat Level 3 message that came in from the Aralsk safe house, which usually meant the safe house was under attack. He hadn't heard from the team and worried Walker and his crew might have been captured.

"What was the exact local time the safe house message came in?" asked General Black of his aide.

"Sir, the Threat Level 3 message came in at exactly 1255 Aralsk local time—not too long after your call to Colonel Walker. If I were Colonel Walker, I'd hide out until dark and then hot-start a vehicle. If the Russians are looking for a radio transmission, he'll have to wait until clear of Aralsk."

"Point taken," said General Black to his aide. "We'll need to monitor the emergency Iridium channel in case they attempt to contact us. It won't be dark there for another seven hours."

28

AS SOON AS they all got to the abandoned flower shop, Jared and Rick set up a perimeter defense. Walker watched for anyone following them. Sure enough, one of the soldiers popped his head out of the back door of the pharmacy.

"Jared, is there an attic or basement in this building?" Walker asked.

"Boss, I didn't look yet—I'll check right now."

"Hurry! We don't have much time."

Jared ran upstairs, checking out each floor. Susan noticed a large section of the wall in the main room had warped pretty badly.

"That wall is really warped," she said to Walker. "Maybe it goes to an old storage area."

"I'll check it out; you and Vladimir stay low. They might see us through the front window."

Walker checked out the bulging wall; it was really a wallpapered door. He ran a knife blade through the wallpaper and pulled on the edge. The door opened to a dark stairway descending to a basement.

"Mac, good call. There's an old stairway to a basement room. Stay here while I go check it out. Rick, watch for any visitors coming our way. Shoot to kill."

Jared came back down the stairway. "Boss, the upstairs used to be a living quarters—no attic."

Walker returned from the basement. "Everyone, quickly, grab your stuff; we're goin' to the basement—now! Rick, JD, we'll need the headlamps when we get down there."

Walker, Rick, and Jared set up a point defense at the bottom of the stairs. It was dark and dirty, and Susan looked around for a place to hide. The basement had clearly been used as a storage area because there were eight very large boxes resembling miniature freighter storage containers with their doors open. Each was large enough to hold four people.

"Here's the plan. We need to stack these up against the wall so the goons will give up looking inside every container. Rick, JD, push these against the wall into the corner. Vladimir and Mac will get in that one and then Brian and Rick will move another into place. Then Rick and Brian will get in the second one. JD and I will move the rest in close proximity and get into the third one. We'll make the doors extremely difficult to open. Let's get moving! Once inside, turn off all light sources and anything that could make a sound. Close the door, but don't lock it. If you hear shots fired, then JD and I have been found. Hopefully, it won't end well for the Russians."

The containers were relatively clean inside except for a few spiders and other dead bugs. The door seals were rubber and would cut off all oxygen, so they couldn't stay in them for very long. One by one, each container was moved into position with the door difficult to open unless each container was moved and rotated. Susan felt something moving at her feet.

"Vladimir, do you feel that?"

Vladimir turned on his pocket LED. "Just a couple field mice," he said.

Susan shrieked, "I hate those things."

"Don't worry, they'll leave us alone."

In less than ten minutes, they heard footsteps at the top of the stairway. Two Russian soldiers slowly came down the stairs with their flashlights and pistol laser beams on. After a brief check of the basement, they holstered their weapons, pulled out the first of the eight containers, opened the door, looked inside, and started pulling out the seventh, sixth, and fifth in progression, looking inside each one.

Walker whispered to Jared, "Four down and one to go."

As they got to the fifth container, a voice on one of their radios called out, "Search status?"

One of the soldiers yelled back on their radio. "This place looks like a storage facility for dead bodies! No one yet."

On the other end of the radio, "Forget it. We need you back up here searching other buildings." The soldiers finished inspecting the fifth container, saw that it was empty, and started back up the stairs.

"That was close. Let's sit tight for a few more minutes," Walker whispered.

Director Arkonov was getting nervous. So far, no Americans found. He radioed the field team commander, Major Golubkin.

"How is the search progressing?"

"Director, the search is progressing well; we have searched all the local buildings and are widening the search into the countryside. If they are here, we will find them."

"Did you set up blockades on all the roads leading into and out of Aralsk?" asked the director.

"Yes sir, the roads are blocked. No one can come in or out without an inspection."

"Well done, Commander. Call me with an update every ten minutes."

About five minutes after the two soldiers left, Walker whispered to JD, "Pop your head out and check the area. Shoot to kill."

Jared screwed the silencer on his Glock and then, as quietly as possible, exited the container and poked his head above the containers in front of his. He climbed over the remaining containers, Glock in hand, until he got to the foot of the stairs. He faintly heard commands being called out and decided to wait and listen for a few minutes. When the search team had moved on, he called out.

"Boss, the search squad has left the area."

Walker pushed the door open against the second container, came out, and banged on the other two containers. "All clear!"

"We're playing a deadly game of hide-and-seek," Susan said. "What if they come back?"

"You're right. We just dodged a bullet!"

"So, Colonel Walker, what is our plan?" Vladimir asked.

"We lay low, stay here until nightfall, then steal a vehicle and drive to the next safe house."

"Where is the next safe house anyway?" asked Rick.

"It's in a harbor town on the Ural River called Atyrau," answered Walker.

"That's a fifteen-hour drive," Vladimir said. "I think I will take my chances and head back to my horse ranch."

"The FSB might have seen your face and eventually arrest you as a traitor," warned Walker. "But if you really want to go back, do it under cover of darkness—tonight. Whatever you need from us, we'll provide. We never could have executed this op without you. If you change your mind and decide to defect, that works too! Anyway, we need to stay put until nightfall and then JD and Rick will look for transportation. Did anyone see any food in the pharmacy?"

"I think there was a small snack food stand—hopefully healthy stuff," Susan recalled.

"Usually, aptekas carry protein drinks and meal replacements," said Vladimir.

"Rick, JD, scout out the pharmacy and see what food and drinks you can bring back, and be careful not to be seen."

Jared and Rick, both armed with their silenced Glock 19s, slowly went up the stairs.

"Sir, what can I do?" asked Brian.

"Plot the road trip to Atyrau, including distances between major centers or intersections," said Walker. "In particular, we need to call back to Center on the satphone as soon as possible to let them know we're okay. We need to start comm discipline because I think the FSB is tracking satcom on the ground."

Jared and Rick returned a few minutes later with handfuls of food and drinks.

Four hours had passed and the FSB director was getting impatient with reports of no one found or captured. At the last check-in, the field commander, Golubkin, said the Americans had somehow slipped out of town.

"They may have split up so as not to raise suspicion."

"Commander Golubkin, you need to redouble your efforts! If you need more soldiers, let me know. I don't think I need to emphasize the importance of finding and capturing these Americans. They are crafty and dangerous, so try thinking like them. What would they do in this situation?"

"Director, sir, if I were them, I would lie low until dark and then attempt to escape."

"I agree. Make sure any vehicle that appears out of place is stopped and searched . . . and continue the search through the night."

"We will need a second shift," said the commander.

"Commander, I will send more people to help, including one of my top agents—Nikolai Maksim. He is specially trained to hunt people down. Capturing these spies is the highest priority of the FSB."

"Eat and drink what you can, but save some for the trip. Blame Rick and JD for this excellent food selection. Leave reasonable tips please!" Walker joked.

"There was actually some healthy stuff in there!" Susan said.

It was nearly dusk and Walker readied the team. "As soon as the town lights come on, JD and Rick will scour the town for a van, truck, or other large vehicle for us all to fit in. Make sure the tank is full before you boost it." Walker turned to Vladimir. "So, what have you decided?"

"I appreciate the offer and the assistance, but I really love my ranch and I want to get back to it. I will find my way back—I may need some extra Kazakhstani tenge to pay my way back."

"That's no problem. Brian is our banker."

"I have enough tenge to buy a city! Here you go."

Brian started counting out the three million tenge for Vladimir.

"Now I can buy more political favors as well," Vladimir said. "Thank you, and I wish all of you the best of luck. *Do svidaniya*, my friends."

Before Vladimir started up the stairs, Rick asked if he needed a weapon or ammo.

"No, I have my trusty Baikal 441 and five eight-round magazines. Thanks for the offer. You know where to find me." And with that, Vladimir Ivanov left the abandoned flower shop and headed south to Baikonur on foot, in the dark.

Keeping good comm discipline was an absolute necessity, but Walker was anxious to get word back to HQ that they had escaped the safe house attack and were on the run.

"Brian, think we could risk a short message burst back to HQ? We should be okay now, right?"

"Colonel, the only means of communication that would not be intercepted would be carrier pigeon. We really shouldn't transmit until we are out of Aralsk."

"Roger that," said a reluctant Walker.

With full darkness now over the town, Walker decided it was time to make a move.

"Rick, you and JD go topside, find a good-sized van or truck, and make sure it has a full tank!"

"Boss, do you want me to put down temblors in case an intruder comes along?" Rick asked.

"No, I won't know if it's you two or an intruder. Before either of you come down the stairs, just call out 'Labrador retriever' so we'll know it's you. Good luck."

Rick and Jared checked their Glocks, silencers, MP-5s, and extra magazines, and headed upstairs.

Jared and Rick swung slowly behind the neighboring buildings with a watchful eye toward the main street. Periodically, they heard commands yelled off in the distance.

"I guess they think we left the village and ran through the woods," Rick said.

Jared agreed. "It sounds like they're way outside of the village searching the wooded areas."

As they made their way around the few business buildings in town, they spotted what appeared to be a fairly large garage. As they approached it, they noticed a familiar symbol of crossed axes on a shield on the building—a fire station house. There were two vehicles inside, an emergency rescue vehicle and a large fire truck. The house seemed to be empty; they looked all around the building for any lights inside.

"The place looks empty, so maybe we can just boost the fire truck," Rick said.

"I think we should take the emergency rescue vehicle," Jared said. "It has plenty of room for five, including someone on the stretcher."

"Emergency vehicle it is," said Rick.

They approached the side entrance, and Jared noticed a low light coming from one of the back rooms. "I think someone might be here."

Rick whispered, "Check out the room; if there's someone there, take them out."

"I don't think the boss wants us to engage anyone if we can avoid contact," answered Jared.

"Okay, you take the lead. If things go south, you'll have to take care of business."

Jared nodded, started toward the lighted room, and then they both saw an old man asleep on a cot.

"Leave him; get the keys from the main office," Rick whispered.

Rick looked for an office area, found it, then searched for keys to the rescue vehicle.

"When you find the keys, we open the garage door, push the vehicle out, close the doors, then start the truck," Jared said softly. "They won't know it's missing until morning."

Rick noticed a mini cabinet on the wall, but it was padlocked. "Check to see if there's a bolt cutter on the fire truck?"

"Shit—we need a bolt cutter? Now?" asked Jared.

"If you don't want to jump-start the truck with the ignition wires, then yes!" said Rick.

Just as Jared moved to check the fire truck for a bolt cutter, Rick was startled.

"Who is there?" someone said in Kazakhstani. "Is that you, Ganibek?"

Both Jared and Rick stayed out of sight, but the old guy was not going to let it go. Rick waited until the old man was in the office and then pounced on him and hit him hard with the butt of the Glock. The man crumpled to the floor unconscious. Rick tied him up with wire from the desk phone. He put a piece of cloth in his mouth and put tape from the desk around his head and over the cloth and took his ID.

With the situation under control, Jared grabbed the bolt cutter from the fire truck and ran to the office.

"Where's the padlock? Did you kill him?"

Rick pointed to the small wall cabinet and said, "No, just knocked him out."

Jared cut the lock off. "Holy crap, there are five key sets in here. How do we pick the right ones?"

"Try 'em all," Rick whispered.

"Look for extra rescue personnel uniforms and IDs—we'll need them," said Jared as he headed to the rescue truck. He found the right keys with the third set, started the truck, but noticed that the tank was just half full.

"Shit, the tank's not full, but we need to get the hell out of here. Are there any gas cans in the garage?"

Rick threw the uniforms and the few ID badges he found into the truck and then looked around for a gas can.

"I found one that's half full; better than nothing!" Rick opened the garage door and Jared pulled out onto the driveway. Rick closed the garage door, then jumped into the rescue vehicle, whispering, "Let's go—but quietly!"

"I'll inch our way back to the flower shop and pull into the closest driveway."

Jared quietly pulled into the driveway, and then killed the engine. They jumped out, weapons drawn, Jared leading and Rick checking the rear as they walked to the back of the building. At the top of the stairs, Jared whispered, "Labrador retriever!"

The FSB director got a call from Major Golubkin, commander of the search crew. "Nikolai has arrived at the safe house and has decided to start with the original escape path. He prefers to work alone, so he will check in with me periodically."

"That is why I sent him; he is like a bloodhound. You should assign one of your soldiers to follow him just in case."

"Director, sir, he has refused any assistance and has promised to report in every hour."

"Fine, let him go on his own. But if he fails to call in every hour, let me know. I will call him personally."

Walker was relieved to hear the impromptu codeword from his tactical team.

"Boss, we got a rescue vehicle and some rescue personnel uniforms with IDs," Jared reported. "Unfortunately, the tank wasn't full, but we've got a spare gas can."

"I had to clock the firehouse keeper to shut him up. I don't think we need to worry about him," Rick added.

"Nice work," said Walker. "You guys were gone longer than expected. Everyone, pick out a rescue outfit and put it on."

As they put the uniforms on, Rick's phone indicated the tunnel temblor sensor had triggered.

"Boss, someone's coming through the tunnel. I think we have company."

"Shit, they decided to retrace our steps?"

Jared heard the back door being pried open, and whispered, "Quiet! I heard something upstairs." A few seconds later, they heard footsteps. Jared whispered to Walker, "Sounds like one person."

Walker whispered back, "You two, get behind the stairs and take out the intruder. We'll stay hidden behind the second container. Go!"

They heard the intruder walk around upstairs. A few minutes later the intruder started walking down the stairs—slowly. Jared waved at Rick to shoot first. It was dark down there since there was no light source and they left their NVGs in the safe house. As soon as the intruder got to the next to last step, Rick fired two rounds from the Glock—one into his back and the other into his leg. The intruder fired two rounds into the floor as he crumpled to the basement floor.

Jared ran to him and saw that he was still alive. The intruder had NVGs and a Kevlar vest on. The back shot was slowed by the vest but penetrated the kidney area. It was the leg shot that took him down. He was writhing on the floor. Jared quickly shoved a ripped piece of his shirt into the man's mouth, and then put his hands and feet into zip ties.

He took the intruder's NVGs and searched for a second weapon while Rick picked up the weapon he dropped— an MP-443 Grach with an eighteen-round box magazine and an attached laser that was turned off. Rick found a holstered Makarov PM inside the vest as well as a cell phone and high-powered walkie-talkie.

"He's not wearing a uniform like the others," Walker said.

"His ID says he's FSB, but the rest is in Russian military code," Rick said, handing the ID to Walker.

"Nikolai Maksim. He's a special operator for FSB—probably ex-Spetsnaz. This guy could be dangerous," Walker said, putting the ID in his pocket.

A few minutes later, the writhing stopped. "Check for a pulse."

"He's dead," Rick said.

"Strip him of everything he's wearing just in case he has an emergency beacon," Walker said. When they were done, Rick and Jared shoved the corpse into a container, grabbed the man's cell phone and the walkie-talkie, and put a zip tie through the container door hasp.

"Let's hope this guy worked alone. JD, Rick, you two lead the way!"

They all bounded up the stairs, loaded down with their gear.

29

AFTER THEY LOADED into the rescue vehicle and dressed the part, Brian plotted their escape using the DoD's GPS. The roads leaving Aralsk would have roadblocks, so Walker, who could speak fluent Russian, decided to drive. Brian looked up the address of the nearest hospital in the direction of their escape.

"Sir, there's a small medical center in the city of Shalkar north and west of Aralsk, which is on our planned escape route. They do minor medical procedures like broken bones, serious cuts and abrasions, like from vehicle accidents. We're in a Class 3 specialty ambulance, so we would be the first on the scene of an accident."

Walker yelled into the back, "Rick, Mac, make it appear that JD was in an accident and has a broken arm and is bleeding from the head. Keep your sidearms at the ready and make sure you can get to your MP-5s in case things go sideways."

"Roger that, boss," yelled out Rick.

"Do they have female EMTs here? I don't speak either Kazakh or Russian," Susan said.

"Yeah, I know—and neither does Jared. Just let Rick do the talking."

Walker knew there was a better than 50 percent chance that if they got stopped, they would wind up in a shootout. He hoped that the soldiers at the roadblock were inexperienced.

Walker looked down the road. "Okay, everybody, there's a roadblock ahead with bright lights. We need to look like we're carrying an emergency patient. Be sharp! If I yell out *idti* twice, that means 'go' in Russian, and we'll need to shoot our way out."

Susan panicked. "Shoot our way out? I don't even have a weapon! What am I supposed to do?"

"Rick and I will take the heat," Jared said. "Just get low and duck."

"Mac, Rick and JD have experience with these situations. Just do your best impersonation of an EMT in an emergency situation," Walker added.

Susan put a breathing mask over Jared's face and started wrapping bandages around his head. She poured red chlorohexidine on the bandages and got out a stethoscope. About 300 yards out, Walker put on his siren and then, as they got in line, one soldier started toward their truck. Walker turned the siren off and the soldier came alongside his door.

The soldier said in Russian, "ID! Now!" Walker pulled out Nikolai's ID, handed it to the guard, and said, in Russian, "I am Nikolai Maksim. We have an accident victim from a government vehicle that crashed on M32. We need to get him to the medical center at Shalkar. Now!"

The soldier waved him on. "Go around the line and pull up at the lights." Walker nodded and watched as the soldier discussed the situation with someone on his radio.

"Turn on the walkie-talkie that JD took from the FSB agent. Maybe we can listen in," Walker said to Brian.

"Did you check in the back for the victim? Did you check for any other ID? If they really have an emergency, let them go," Walker heard on the radio. "At least we know where they are going. Handle it. Out," said Major Golubkin, still combing the countryside with dogs.

"Act the part, folks," Walker said to his team. "The guard is coming to check the victim in back. Rick, I hope your Russian is good enough!"

The guard yelled into the cab, "Where is your ID—I need to see your ID," pointing to Brian. Brian pulled out the ID of the guy at the fire station and handed it to Walker, who handed it to the guard. The guard did a cursory check and then handed it back to Walker.

"I need to look in back; tell them to open the doors."

"Open the doors; they need to check us out," yelled Walker into the back.

The guard came around, pointing his weapon into the back. "What happened to him?"

Rick replied in his best Russian, "He collided with another car on M32. He is stabilized, but we need to get him to the medical center at Shalkar."

Susan put the stethoscope on Jared's chest.

"Get going. Save that guy!" the guard said.

Walker nodded and rode off with the siren blaring.

"We're not out of the woods yet," he said to the team. "There may be another roadblock further up the road. Nice job and stay cool. Rick, pretty good Russian back there! I'll buy the next round of vodka. Brian, listen to the talkie and raise the volume. Maybe we'll catch another break!"

They heard periodic chatter between the roadblock soldiers and the commander. There were three calls asking for his status. About fifteen minutes beyond the roadblock, Nikolai's cell phone rang. The FSB director was calling since Nikolai had not checked in as required.

"Should we answer his phone?" Brian asked.

"No! We're gonna dump it off on another vehicle when we stop for gas."

As they drove toward Atyrau, the harbor city on the Ural River, the time crept by.

"You guys are pretty resourceful," Susan said to the team. "Do you fear anything?"

"I was almost killed or captured in Afghanistan. There's been a few times when I thought it was over for me," said Rick.

"I've been lucky; most of my missions have been in Eastern European countries. An operation in Romania went south and we lost an agent. Our cover was blown and we were almost captured. How about you? Did you ever get into a bad situation?" asked Jared.

"If you don't include this mission, I would say my most dangerous venture was dating a psycho lawyer. He took me to his house on our first date and expected sex. But I'm an old-fashioned kind of gal. I had to practically threaten to pepper spray him before he backed off. Now I'm engaged to a great guy. He's a neurosurgeon and we're planning to get married next year. But I keep the pepper spray handy just in case."

The team laughed. "Thanks for sharing," Jared said.

The walkie-talkie was useless once they were out of range. There were no more roadblocks. After four hours of driving in the dark, they stopped for gas along E-40 in Makat. Everyone got out to stretch their legs.

"Throw the cell phone into the back of that food delivery truck. It's based out of Almaty and probably headed to Baikonur," Walker said to Brian. "Tracking the phone will send them on a wild goose chase for a while." He smirked.

Sure enough, a search party was assembled to track Nikolai Maxim's path after the director again failed to make contact with the agent. Field commander Golubkin retraced Nikolai's steps. After inspecting the basement of the old abandoned flower shop, he noticed blood on the floor. Nikolai's body was found in one of the storage containers—with his ID, cell phone, and radio missing. The field commander timidly called the director.

The FSB director was awakened from a nap in his office. "So, Commander Golubkin, what news do you have? It's almost morning and you should have caught the American spies by now!"

"They must have been hiding in the abandoned flower shop basement. There were many large containers in—"

"Are you telling me that they were missed during the initial search of the town buildings?"

"Yes sir, unfortunately that is the case," said the commander.

"Have you found Nikolai? I have not been able to reach him."

"Nikolai is dead. We found his body in one of the containers."

"Are you sure it's him?"

"Yes sir. His ID, cell, and radio were missing."

"Get his body to the morgue. He deserves a medal for finding the Americans . . . and you deserve to be shot for not finding them. Commander, where are the Americans now?"

"Sir, we think they may have jump-started a car or truck and attempted to escape. But every exit from Aralsk has a roadblock."

"What about side roads, Commander? Are there any leading out of the city?"

"No sir; the terrain is too rough for anything other than an off-road or military vehicle."

"You better be right, Commander."

30

GENERAL BLACK WAS getting impatient.

"So, where are we with the satellite control software? And how close is L2Cnet to getting an aircraft ready to go?"

"General, the L2Cnet Gulfstream G550, with a beam-steering antenna, will be ready to go in five days, but we still need to test the actual telemetry signals in the various control modes. We won't have that ready until tomorrow," Callahan said.

"Excellent! And the rest of the schedule?"

"Sir, the one thing we won't know for sure is whether the encryption algorithm really works."

"Who's the expert on encryption?" asked General Black.

Robbie Chan, the WEBMAZE team's telemetry expert, spoke first. "Although my expertise is in signals intelligence, I know a little about crypto codes."

"Okay, Chan, explain to me why we won't know if the encryption works?"

"Well, sir, the algorithm can be changed at any time by the Russians. As you are aware, the DoD does the same thing. We are presently assuming a monthly rollover of the codes, which is typical for Russian satellite telemetry codes. That means we might be okay for the next two to three weeks."

"Two weeks?" asked General Black. "That's all?"

"Unfortunately, that's when we will need to collect more signals," answered Chan.

"So, now you tell me, if the signals don't work, the crypto algorithm was changed?"

"Robbie is correct," Callahan said. "Unless we know the specific rollover period—or even if there is one—the control signal may or may not work as planned."

"Okay then. But it's now even more of an imperative to get the system functioning within the next week or so. Is that possible?"

"Sir, to the best of our present knowledge of the situation with the Gulfstream, the crypto codes, and the telemetry signals, we think it can be ready in seven days," Callahan said.

"Press hard, Callahan. The field team can't go back. It's now up to you people. We need to control that damn satellite! I want status updates every four hours."

Chan was a bit shocked about the seven days and expressed as much after the general left. "Richard, you know there's a huge risk in that seven-day schedule. I would have gone with something a bit more realistic—like fourteen days."

"We have done it in seven days before, so let's make that our goal."

"Yeah, but that was when we already knew the telemetry format for the orbital commands and the crypto was much simpler," Chan said.

"Okay, everybody—lets shoot for seven days! If we don't think we'll get there, I will personally take the blame and tell the general myself. I guess we'll all be working late the next few days."

"My work is almost done," said Marsha, the space weapons expert. "The telemetry antenna is a narrowband, beam-steering, circularly polarized dome and is ready to go. It's being installed on the Gulfstream tomorrow."

"I should be finished with the three telemetry commands we've deciphered by tomorrow night," Chan said. "It includes 'open the auxiliary antenna arms,' 'close the auxiliary antenna arms,' and 'shift orbit easterly.' I would've liked to have the telemetry data to deorbit or increase apogee, but we'll probably never get that."

It was unanimously decided by the cosmodrome's special weaponized satellite team that because of the success of the first two firings, a bigger test needed to be performed. It was clear from the second test that resistance to the high-powered microwave burst occurred at around fifty feet of depth—at least, of building structure. A good test of depth would be an underground system like a subway system or a mine.

It would be easiest to verify the effectiveness of penetration at an underground subway, so that was the choice. Next to consider: where. It had to appear random and not raise suspicion. The London Underground was chosen—specifically the intersection of the Blue Line (Victorian), Red Line (Central), and Brown Line (Bakerloo) at Oxford Circus. The test would be scheduled in two days, at the height of commuter use—around four in the afternoon, with agents monitoring all three tube stations. The countdown started, and so did the commands to change orbit. But this time, there would be no monitoring of the signals by the AQUADUCT team.

Callahan got the report from the satellite monitoring folks at NRO that Cosmos 2455 was shifting orbits again, then shared that with the team.

"Cosmos 2455 must have an exceptional orbital change fuel load," said DuBois. "That puts the orbit over London— one of the major cities that could be targeted! Maybe we should warn MI6 to watch for a potential localized EMP event, something that might not normally raise suspicion."

"We need to tell General Black now," Callahan said. "He can decide what to do. Let's go."

"General Black, we just received the new orbital path for Cosmos 2455, and it appears to be shifting its track over London," Callahan reported. "No other large cities are in its path. Should we let MI6 know?"

"At the present time, there are only three people read into WEBMAZE at MI6, under the code word *WHITEHEAD*. That should be enough to monitor anything suspicious. Pull together the orbital period, overpass times, and what to look for. I will share that with our WHITEHEAD partners right away."

31

DAWN WAS APPROACHING, and after driving for six hours straight, the team was tired and wary of being stopped again.

"Boss, maybe we should ditch this and find new wheels," Brian said.

"We're almost at Kandyagash where A26 intersects A27. We can look for another truck there," Walker said. "Team, we're abandoning this truck and getting a new one. This one's too risky to drive." Walker wished he could just call for an exfil and a Black Hawk to pick them up, but that would be far too risky for the DoD.

Walker decided to check in with General Black. "Okay to go satcom?" he asked Brian.

"Yup. We're far from any cities where the signal could be intercepted."

"Center, this is Agent five, zero, three, Golf, Whiskey, Xray, seven, one. Put me through to General Black."

"Steve, glad to hear your voice. We were worried you and your team might have been captured!"

"The escape was intense for a few hours, but we hid and waited until dark. Everyone's okay, but it's been a tough op, sir. Two safe houses have been attacked and hosts captured or killed. We're on the road to the Atyrau safe house in a stolen rescue vehicle that we plan to dump at the next town."

"The Atyrau safe house agents are expecting your team. Is Vladimir with you?"

"No. Vladimir decided to take the risk and return to his ranch. We'll have to provide a cover story in case he's captured."

"It's his decision and we must respect that—but we'll help where we can. We'll keep monitoring Vladimir's status. Safe travels. Contact us when you are close to the safe house. Center out."

At dawn, the search commander, Golubkin, was approached by a man babbling about a stolen emergency rescue vehicle from their fire station.

"Director, there is a firehouse operator here who says he was knocked out by someone and realized their emergency rescue vehicle was missing when he came to."

"Detain him," Director Arkonov barked. "Get the make, model, year, color, and registration plates. Then send the description to every police station in Kazakhstan. If you can get a picture of it, broadcast that too. I will dispatch a helicopter to search from the air. I suspect there may be another safe house nearby, but someone must have seen that truck by now. I want to know where it is!"

"Yes sir. I will let you know what I find."

The commander asked the man details about the truck and then immediately called each of the blockades. He hit pay dirt at the last blockade on M26/E38 leaving Aralsk.

"Yes sir, there was an emergency rescue vehicle with four emergency staff and one injured person in back. They were all wearing emergency personnel uniforms. They were headed to the medical center at Shalkar. That was over six hours ago."

"They spoke to you in Russian?" asked Commander Golubkin.

"Yes sir. The driver and one of the men in back spoke perfect Russian. The others were quiet."

"Get your team together and drive to Shalkar, now! Find that truck!" He immediately called Director Arkonov.

"Director, sir, the Americans stole an emergency rescue vehicle and got through the blockade," the commander reported. "They said they were bringing an accident victim to Shalkar."

"Did they show their IDs to the blockade sergeants?"

"Yes. Unfortunately, no one closely checked the IDs or the pictures because they looked legitimate."

"Another screwup! Are you searching for that truck?"

"Yes sir. The blockade sergeant has dispatched a search party to Shalkar."

"Good. Let me know if they find the truck."

The WEBMAZE field team was exhausted from driving all night, but they were still on edge about the truck. As they entered Kandyagash, Walker said to Brian, "We need to find a truck that blends in—like a food delivery truck or an electrician's van. Head into the center of town and avoid any police cars."

"Sir, what if we park near the big market over there?" Brian pointed across the street.

"Yeah, go. There might be good places to hide this thing and find a replacement."

As they pulled into the parking lot of an InterFood Supermarket, Brian noticed a police car at the other end of the parking lot. It looked as though he just pulled over another driver and was walking to his car door.

"That was close!" Brian said.

As they drove around the back of the store, Brian and Walker saw a pastry truck at the loading bay. Walker yelled, "Rick, we're parking here. When we stop, get out, go over to the pastry truck and see if the driver left the key in the ignition. Bring the truck over to us. If the driver is nearby, grab him and throw him in. We don't want any loose ends."

"Take him out?" asked Rick.

"No. We just need to make sure that nobody reports the truck missing. Oh, and everyone else except Rick, ditch the rescue squad suits when we stop."

Rick went around the back of the pastry truck. He saw the driver and asked what type of pastries he delivered.

"I have blini, gogol mogul, Kiev cake, pastille, kissel, mille-feuille, and Tula gingerbread. Would you like something?"

"Yes. The mille-feuille sounds good. How much?"

"You an emergency driver?"

"Yes, I work for a fire department."

"Good, then for you, free," the pastry driver said as he stepped into the truck. Rick quickly jumped in behind him, threw him to the floor of the truck, tied his hands and feet with zip ties, and covered his mouth with tape.

In Russian, Rick said, "Sorry, but we need your truck. We will not hurt you, but if you make noise, you will die!"

Rick then jumped into the driver's seat and drove over to the rescue truck.

"Get your stuff and go!" Walker said as Rick pulled alongside and stopped. The team immediately loaded into the pastry truck, Walker riding shotgun, with Brian, Susan, and Jared in the back.

"Who's this guy?" Jared asked.

"He's the witness that can't report the truck heist! He just lent us this fine pastry delivery vehicle," Rick said.

"Nice," yelled Jared. "Now we can eat fine Russian pastry."

"Rick, are you okay to drive?" Walker asked.

"Boss, I had six hours of on-and-off sleep in the back of a rescue truck, so yeah. I'd rather drive anyway."

A few minutes into the drive, Jared took the tape off the captured driver's mouth and asked, "Do you speak English?"

The driver answered, "Yes—little."

"What is your name?" asked Jared.

"Nurlan Erkebulan. I deliver pastries and cakes for Thomi's Pastry."

"Okay, Nurlan. We need to borrow your truck until we get to our next destination. At that time, we will let you go, but you must stay with the truck until someone finds you. Got that?" asked Jared.

"I no want trouble. I do what you say. You Americans?"

"Good guess," answered Jared. "We're being chased by FSB."

"Oooo, bad. FSB captured brother for sneaking on Baikonur Cosmodrome to watch rocket launch. He in ITK long time before let go. Why FSB chasing you Americans?"

"ITKs are corrective labor colonies, in case you were wondering," Rick said.

Jared was reluctant to provide any additional information, so he lied. "We're accused of stealing radios at an electronics store."

"Yes, that bad," Nurlan said. "You in ITK long time."

"We are better than FSB," Jared said. "Get as comfortable as possible; we're driving all the way to Atyrau. I'm sure you won't mind us eating some of your pastries. We'll leave you money for them."

Brian pulled out a wad of tenge and put them in Nurlan's pocket—laughing along with Susan, who, for the first time since the farmhouse incident, felt a sense of relief that they might actually leave Kazakhstan.

The Russian search team entered Shalkar looking for a yellow-and-black emergency rescue vehicle and went straight to the medical center there.

"We are searching for a group of four men and one woman in emergency rescue uniforms. Did you see them?" asked the sergeant in charge of the detail.

"There has been no one here for two days," a receptionist answered. "We sometimes see no one for weeks. Usually we will go treat a local injured farmhand during a farming accident."

"If you happen to see them, call this number."

The sergeant reported to the field commander, who ordered him to do a quick scan of all the vehicles in town. "Keep searching until you run out of towns along A26!"

Commander Golubkin got a call from Director Arkonov.

"We got a call from the Interfood supermarket in Kandyagash that a pastry truck driver just disappeared while delivering his goods. It was black with *Thomi's Pastry* printed on the sides. Get someone out there as fast as you can. Keep an eye out for the rescue vehicle. Call me when you have something!"

Kandyagash was just over five hours from Aralsk but only three hours from Shalkar.

"My search squad in Shalkar verified the Americans did not show up at the medical center there. They can get to Kandyagash in a few hours."

"Send them there immediately, Commander!"

"Yes sir. They are on their way!"

The commander then called his search squad and said, "Sergeant Alexander, this is search commander Major Golubkin; go directly to Kandyagash. The director suspects the American spies are there. Drive as fast as you can! Be on the lookout for the rescue vehicle."

Rick was annoyed that the pastry delivery truck could barely do fifty miles an hour and that it struggled on hills.

"This rattletrap sucks. At this rate, we'll take forever to get to Atyrau!"

Walker agreed. "Just keep the speed as high as possible through the next few towns. We may have to get gas soon; we have about half a tank left."

"Sir, you should contact the general and get the status of the safe house in Atyrau," Brian asked. "It may also be compromised. We are way outside any possible signal intercept zone, so we should be okay to transmit."

"Roger that; I'll contact him now."

"Steve, I was hoping you could check in. We are a few days away from completing our mission thanks to your team. Where are you and what is your status?" General Black asked.

"Sir, we just left Kandyagash in a pastry vehicle and we're on our way to the safe house at Atyrau. Is the safe house clear?"

"Our last contact with them was three hours ago; we can't make contact with them at this time for some unknown reason. All safe houses are on lockdown since Dzhusaly and Aralsk were compromised."

"Sir, we're still about four hours out, so we have some time. We'll call back at ten miles from Atyrau."

"I should know the safe house status by then. Stay alert! Center out."

32

THE FSB DIRECTOR had a good feeling about the noose tightening on the American spies. He directed a helicopter team to search along A26, and they were almost to Kandyagash. He expected a radio report any minute from the lead surveillance helicopter as it approached the Interfood supermarket parking lot. The two Kamov Ka-226T light observation helicopters were fast and fairly quiet.

"Director Arkonov, this is Helo-1 pilot, Anatoly. Sir, we are approaching the Interfood Supermarket parking lot and have spotted the emergency rescue vehicle. There is no activity around the vehicle and the rear doors are open. Do you want us to land and investigate? Over."

"Helo-1—YES! Land close by and verify there are no occupants. Be aware they are armed and dangerous; take no chances. Get a detailed description of the pastry truck the spies commandeered while you are there."

"Yes sir. Helo-1 out."

The Ka-226Ts landed across the street in a field, off-loaded a full FSB Vympel Spetsnaz team, and quickly locked down the rescue vehicle. From his satphone, Captain Evgeny called the director.

"Director, sir, this is Spetsnaz team leader Captain Evgeny—the truck is empty except for rescue vehicle uniforms. We will report back in a few minutes."

FSB director Arkonov figured the Americans couldn't be too far away. Evgeny got back on the radio a few minutes later.

"Sir, the market owner said the pastry truck is owned by Thomi's Pastry of Almaty near the Kyrgystan border. They are most probably in that truck headed to a Caspian Sea port to escape."

"You are probably correct. Get back on the helo and search for the truck. You may need to cover the two main roads along the Caspian, A27 and A33."

"Director, we are in pursuit. Evgeny out."

Walker was hoping for good news about the safe house.

"When we get to Atyrau, we're parking the truck as close to a port facility as possible. They'll find it pretty fast since it's a big target, but it fits into the harbor scene, so not too suspicious. Mac, JD, Brian—we'll drop you three off near the safe house—assuming it's secure. Rick and I will hide the truck and circle back. Keep as much of the mission equipment as possible. Leave behind the MP-5s, ammo, batteries, and other useless crap. Rick and I will dump it in the harbor. Got it?"

"Why don't we just destroy the mission equipment too?" Brian asked. "It's no longer needed."

"I want the hardware and software with me," Susan said. "It'll come in handy during the technical debrief!"

"Brian—I'd agree if we had heavy equipment. So, no, we're not destroying any of our mission equipment except the antennas. I agree with Susan—bring everything mission-related with you."

"Roger that, but my concern was we'd be wide open for attack walking to the safe house," Brian said.

"You'd be right if we're walking—but we're taking taxis to the safe house," Walker said. He didn't want to give any clues as to the whereabouts of the safe house or its name because he wasn't sure how much English their captive guest, Nurlan, understood.

Walker and Rick both saw the sign that Atyrau was 15 km ahead and thus in the window for the safe house status check. Walker first made sure the speaker option was off and then hit the recall memory key.

"Steve, great to hear you made it to Atyrau. NSA has picked up lots of chatter about your team. They're searching everywhere along the coastline, so be careful. All is okay at the safe house, which, as you recall, is underneath the Taksim Café next to the Enrico Marielli store off Abay Street. Make sure to ask for Andrei; he's the safe house captain. He's expecting you. When you meet Andrei, say, in Russian, 'The coffee at Starbucks is too strong. I need a menu.' Andrei will counter in English with 'Starbucks makes pretty good chai tea.' The place is run by safe house agents. They'll get you on a boat that'll bring you to the Caspian where a trawler with Ukrainian flags will be waiting."

"Good news, sir. We're about ten minutes from Atyrau. The plan is to dump the truck and excess baggage and then on to the safe house."

"Sounds like a plan. If things go sideways, destroy everything mission related. So, keep the mini thermites just in case. I'll update you on Cosmos 2455 when you're at the safe house."

"Will do, sir. Out." Walker turned to Jared. "JD, keep the mini thermite grenades—just in case."

"I hate to give up the MP5s, but yes, sir, the thermites are with me."

"Stay sharp; we're less than ten minutes from Atyrau, assuming this rattletrap of a delivery truck makes it!"

"Boss, this is the worst piece of crap I have ever driven—and I've driven a lot of crap," Rick said.

"Sorry, Nurlan—no offense meant, but this rattletrap is a piece of junk," said Jared.

Nurlan laughed. "This truck is dog. Need maintenance two times for a week. You lucky no breakdown so far."

They entered Atyrau from the north, then headed south to Abay Street. Jared readied the MP-5s, ammo, and other miscellaneous boat anchors for ditching. The rest of the equipment was put into boxes that were emptied of the pastries they had all come to appreciate.

"Boss, can we keep some of the pastries?" Jared joked.

"Save some to put on top of the equipment to hide it!"

"Edible camo. That works for me, boss."

"Tie up Nurlan securely, put tape over his mouth, and make sure he can't get free. Sorry, Nurlan," Walker said.

Nurlan mumbled something in Kazakhstani that resembled, "Not again?"

"Slight change of plan," said Walker. "We'll be dropping off you three in the back at the Green Hotel along Abay. After we dump the truck, along with Nurlan, we'll get a taxi back there to meet you. We'll blend in as travelers in the area."

Everything seemed to be going as planned. After a quick visual scan of the area, they dropped off Brian, Susan, and Jared with their boxes of pastries at the Green Hotel. The three looked the part of a special delivery service crew. Walker and Rick then drove to the Ural River Bridge that led to the loading docks. After driving one sweep around the waterfront, they parked in an obscure location near the water's edge away from buildings.

Rick opened the rear door and pulled out the box of MP-5s and ammo, headlamps, NVGs, batteries and chargers, temblors, antennas, and other stuff Jared and Rick had been lugging around. They walked to the edge of the river and threw the stuff in, looking around to make sure that no one was watching. They got back into the pastry van and drove over to a parking area near a taxi stand, which was next to a large building. They backed into a loading dock so that the building partially obscured the truck.

Rick made sure Nurlan's hands and feet were bound tight and that he was unable to kick or make noise. "Someone will find you soon enough—just sit tight."

They got out, locked up the truck, and went to the taxi stand. They were there for only five minutes when a taxi pulled up.

"Do you speak English?" Walker asked.

The driver answered, in English, "Americans! Why, of course! I know five languages. Where would you like to go?"

"The Green Hotel on the other side of the river."

"That will be seven hundred and forty tenge, or four dollars American if you have that," said the driver.

"We will give you thirty-five hundred tenge if you get us there in five minutes," said Walker.

"Hop in and put on your seatbelts." Four minutes and thirty seconds later, they were pulling in front of the Green Hotel.

"You did well; here's five thousand tenge for keeping your word!"

"Thank you, Americans! Call me anytime!" They grabbed their bags and jumped out.

As the taxi drove off, they were met by the rest of the team.

"We need to cross Abay and walk down the side street to the parking area next to the Taksim Café," Walker said.

"Director, this is Helo-1, come in."

"Helo-1, this is the director. Have you found the pastry van yet?"

"Director, this is Anatoly in Helo-1. Not yet. We are searching the waterfront at Aktau and do not see any sign of a Pastry Van. Helo-2 is almost at Atyrau and will report in at any moment. Helo-1 out."

"Helo-1, keep searching for the van. It is likely either at Aktau or Atyrau." Director Arkonov contacted the other helicopter. "Helo-2, this is the director. Are you at Atyrau yet?"

"Director, this is Boris in Helo-2. We are still a few minutes out. We will call back when we find something. Helo-2 out."

The FSB director was now confident that the Americans would be caught within the hour.

"Sergeant Alexander, this is Director Arkonov, come in."

"Director, this is Sergeant Alexander. We are thirty minutes from Kandyagash."

"Sergeant, the American spies have stolen another vehicle—a pastry truck with the words *Thomi's Pastry* on the side. Continue past Kandyagash and go direct to Atyrau."

Walker and the team started the fifteen-minute walk to the Taksim Café, looking like a bizarre crew of pastry salespeople on a march. When they got to the front door, Walker said, "Wait here and I'll meet with Andrei."

Walker opened the door, stepped in, and asked one of the workers for Andrei—in Russian. The worker turned to a person a few feet away and said, in Russian, "Andrei, someone for you."

The man walked over to Walker and said, "Welcome" in English. Walker said, in Russian, "The coffee at Starbucks is too strong. I need a menu."

"Starbucks makes pretty good chai tea . . . Where is the rest of your team?" asked Andrei in Russian.

"Just outside," said Walker in Russian, waving them in.

Andrei noticed that Brian, Susan, and Jared were carrying pastries in boxes. "Are these gifts for the safe house agents?" asked Andrei in English.

"Of course," Jared said. "We Americans never show up empty handed."

They all entered an elevator and, after Andrei entered a code on a small cypher panel, they descended two floors down—even though there was only one B on the button panel. They had descended to an unlabeled sub-basement. At the end of a fifteen-foot hallway was a large door with an electronic key code panel. Andrei entered the key code and the door unlocked. They went in and the door locked behind them.

"Welcome to the Atyrau safe house! Make yourselves at home."

"We've been on the run for almost a week now," Walker said. "It's nice to stop and breathe! Where's the STE room? I need to make a call."

"And where's the lady's room? I need to get cleaned up," Susan said.

Andrei pointed to a room across the hall. Susan put down her box and bolted for the bathroom.

"Is there a kitchen or food prep area?" Brian asked.

"Yeah, and what kinds of food do you have?" asked Rick.

Before Andrei could answer, Jared asked, "Do you guys have beer or liquor down here?"

Andrei showed Walker where the STE room was and said, "Dial-out instructions are on the table."

"Was your cover as pastry delivery people?" Andrei asked.

"Actually, no," Brian said. "We just needed to hide our electronic equipment and pistols. You're welcome to have the pastries now that we're in the safe house! It's from Thomi's."

"Thomi's? That's much better pastry than some of the, how do you say it in American, crap we sell here!" Andrei looked at Walker with a serious expression and said, "I will need to brief you and your team on emergency exit procedures and the defensive system we have in place."

"Roger that, Andrei. We'll be 'all ears' in a few minutes," said Walker as he headed into the STE room.

"Steve!" General Black boomed into the STE. "You made it to the safe house. Your team intact?"

"Sir, we're all here safe and sound. Andrei was ready for us as you said."

The general wanted to boast a little. "The Taksim Café is one of our most recent upgrades. It has two double-walled isolation rooms, a new, lighted escape path, three full-coverage multimode video cameras, and a metal detection system that can detect a weapon as small as a pistol. Every agent at the café is trained in close combat arms and carries a hidden Walther PPKS in 380 auto."

"Sir, at this point, I'd like the team to get at least one good night's sleep and a shower. We've been on the run for over six days now. Susan says she's in adventure overload. Have you heard anything from Vladimir? Did he make it back to his horse ranch? And how far along is the WEBMAZE counter-weapon system?"

"Callahan is busting his team's ass. They already have a G550 ready to go and only needed the final telemetry signals to be programmed into the system. It should be ready to fly in a few days. Susan and Captain Mathers did a fantastic job getting the telemetry data! Personally, thank them for me. It appears the Russians already performed some live testing, so the timeline is critical. And, yes, Vladimir did make it back, and so far no one suspects him."

"Glad to hear Vladimir is okay. I'll relay your personal thanks to Brian and Susan. Unless there's a hitch, we'll be on our way to the Caspian in the morning for the exfil. Anything else, sir?"

"Not at this time. Stay in the game and safe travels tomorrow. Oh, I just remembered—Vladimir asked if we could buy a replacement truck for his friends, the Ospanovs? Tell me more about that later. Center out."

"He's a good guy. Agent out."

"Director Arkonov, this is Helo-2."

"Helo-2, what is your status?"

"This is Boris in Helo-2. Nothing yet, sir. We have flown along the Ural River and scanned both the loading docks and shopping areas and nothing yet."

"Helo-2, keep the search going. Helo-1 will be there to assist in the search. Director out."

"Helo-2 out."

"Helo-1, this is the director. Are you close to Atyrau? Helo-2 needs assistance in the search."

"Director, this is Anatoly in Helo-1. Sir, we are about twenty-five minutes out. We will coordinate the search with Helo-2 when we arrive."

"Helo-1, stick to that plan. The Americans most likely are somewhere in Atyrau. Director out."

The director then pulled out his iridium satphone and dialed.

"Sergeant Alexander, what is your status?"

"Director, we are about three hours out but keeping our speed. We had to refuel and get food for the troops. Any other orders?"

"Sergeant, press hard for Atyrau. There was no sign of them at Aktau, so we suspect they are at Atyrau. Let me know when you get to Atyrau. Out."

"Yes sir; out."

33

THE TAKSIM CAFÉ safe house was well designed: full security, excellent lighting, large kitchen, weapons room, game room, STE/Comm room, a conference center, ten bedrooms, men's and women's bathrooms with full showers, and a workout room. There was plenty of food and drink, and a good night's sleep was now almost guaranteed. A change of clothing was offered and accepted—they could finally get out of their dressy cover-story wear, which was getting a bit dank and smelly. Andrei made sure everyone knew the emergency escape procedures and the intruder alert signals. He put all their weapons in a storage area and readied them with matched ammo loads. Per Susan and Brian's request, Andrei provided hermetically sealed cases for the mission electronics that they immediately prepared for the trip.

Although the agents there were all trained in close combat arms, Walker suspected that none on the safe house team had ever actually been under attack. He also knew that due to the mandatory isolation between safe house operators, the Taksim agents had no idea about the fall of the safe houses in Dzhusaly and Aralsk.

"These guys seem inexperienced," Walker told Rick and Jared. "If the FSB finds them, they'll panic. I suggest we keep our pistols nearby tonight, just in case."

"Roger that, boss," said Rick. "These guys are newbies and would crack under fire."

"I was gonna do that anyway," Jared said. "After what happened at Dzhusaly and Aralsk, I don't believe these agents would survive a full-scale FSB attack."

"I will tell Andrei so he doesn't get freaked out at the exfil meeting later," said Walker.

Andrei came by and reminded everyone to meet in the conference room for the exfil brief. As they showed up, Andrei noticed that Jared, Rick, and Walker were toting their Glocks.

"You guys don't trust us? We've been loyal to the CIA and would never compromise you guys."

"It's not that we don't trust you; we've been through some bad situations that called for quick trigger pulls," Walker said.

"I understand," said Andrei. "We were running a different safe house six years ago and the FSB stumbled onto us. It got kind of messy since we were playing like a Russian mafia organization and had to, how do you say it in America, 'Grease a few palms.' We unfortunately lost one of our men in the short gun battle, but they did too. They realized we had some influence and money, and wanted in. We still pay them to look the other way, but they have no idea that the old safe house is just a ruse. We meet there twice a month for show. The CIA gave us a lot of money to build this safe house and it is a really good one."

"We heard the same thing from our people," Walker said, winking at Jared and Rick.

After Walker heard that story, he changed his mind about Andrei's team. Andrei started explaining the exfil plan.

After the plan was briefed, Walker said, "I need to get back on the STE before we hit the hay."

"Steve, everything okay? You should've gotten your exfil briefing by now. Ready to go?" asked the general.

"Sir, in fact we are. But I'm concerned that we may be outgunned if we're spotted on the open sea. Can you coordinate a backup special ops force to assist us in the event we're under attack? If we get to the Caspian Sea and international waters, the Russians will probably back down."

"That's a tall order since the closest SOF troops are stationed at Incirlik, Turkey, and they'll take too long to get to the northern Caspian. I'll talk with the SOCOM commander there and see what he can set up. We're friendly with Azerbaijan. Maybe they'll let us pre-position on their coast. That usually means they'll expect a favor in return."

"Sir, I've done exfils for almost eight years, and after all the close calls on this op, this exfil might be our toughest."

"I understand. I will go with your gut on this. What time tomorrow morning is the exfil?"

"We're assembling at 0600 and should be on their river boat by 0800. The SOF team must get to the northern Caspian no later than 0845."

"Let me see what I can do, but I think you'll be pleasantly surprised by Andrei's boat."

"Any combat assets would be appreciated. Out."

The general thought, *I have an idea.*

The two Ka-226Ts zigzagged through Atyrau—Helo-1 from north to south, Helo-2 from south to north.

"Helo-2, this is Helo-1. Present position?"

"Helo-1, this is Helo-2. We are just north of Sultan Baybarys Ave headed west over the Ural River."

"Helo-2, stay on your present search cycle. Pay close attention to parking lots near the harbors along the Ural River. Helo-1 out."

"Helo-1, we have about thirty-five minutes of fuel remaining."

"Helo-2, we have only about forty-five minutes of fuel, so we will continue our search. We will meet you at the Atyrau International Airport and refuel."

Director Arkonov realized that the airport would be the ideal escape route, so he called the airport security chief.

"This is FSB director Vasilly Arkonov. We need your assistance in capturing five Americans that may be planning to fly out of Atyrau International. I will be sending you a picture of them. Do you have a picture phone?"

"Director, this is Chief of Security Pyotr Konstantin. Yes, I do have a picture phone." He gave the director his number.

"Chief, you should get the picture in a few minutes. Let me know when you get it. These Americans are armed and dangerous, so be careful."

It was getting late, and darkness would hamper the search, so Arkonov called the search team.

"Sergeant Alexander, it is getting late, so it might be best if your team coordinates the ground search with the local police. Go to the Atyrau Police headquarters and request their assistance."

"Yes sir, we are on our way now. We have not yet heard from Anatoly in Helo-1, but we will coordinate with him as well. Alexander out."

"Work with the locals to search for the pastry truck and the American spies. Director out."

Director Arkonov knew the Americans were likely in Atyrau getting help for an escape out of Kazakhstan. With the airport being monitored, the next most likely escape routes would be by train or ship. He needed to cover the exit to the Caspian Sea via the Ural River. He needed Sergeant Alexander to get a search team situated along the exit of the Ural River to the Caspian Sea and one at each train station leaving Kazakhstan.

"Seargeant Alexander, this is Director Arkonov. Come in."

"Sir, this is Sergeant Alexander. Over."

"Sergeant, set up a surveillance team downstream near the mouth of the river and make sure the railroad stations are covered."

"Do you want us to set up a fast boat too?"

"Yes. Get two fast boats, each with a Kalashnikov PKM and RPGs. Director out."

Sergeant Alexander was told to search all the parking areas along the waterfront areas in town. The helo pilots said they had not spotted the pastry truck from the air and had only enough time and fuel to stay airborne another thirty minutes. They were through for the day.

"Sergeant Alexander, this is Anatoly in Helo-1. What's your status?"

"FSB director Arkonov wants us to coordinate with the local police to keep the search going all night. He also wants us to set up a surveillance team along the Ural River and put a fast boat at the exit to the Caspian."

"Sergeant, your team will be busy until late this evening. I will contact you at 0600 when we resume our search. Call us if you find the truck. Helo-1 out."

General Black's only WEBMAZE contact was Michael Hunter, chief at MI6, known to the public as the Secret Intelligence Service, or SIS—Britain's equivalent of the CIA. Via STE, General Black initiated contact.

"Sir Michael, this is General Black. We need to talk."

Chief Hunter recognized his voice right away. "General Joe Black, my American friend at arms. To what do I owe the pleasure?"

General Black got right to the point. "Sir Michael, I realize it is late there, but the WEBMAZE team here has been busy with a new Russian satellite, Cosmos—"

The chief broke in. "Cosmos 2455, right, old boy?"

A bit surprised, General Black asked, "So, your folks are tracking it too?"

"Of course. We have been tracking it since it was launched, and we do not believe it is a Russian communication satellite."

"You're right. We've determined that it's an HPM weapon system. We believe it's been operationally tested twice already. In fact, that's why I'm calling. We believe they might soon attempt a third test over Britain since the orbit crosses over London."

"The bloody Russians are at it again! I will set up monitoring around London to look for unexplained attacks against electronics. Let me know what we can do to help. Can you share your plans?"

"We're still characterizing the satellite's capabilities and datalinks. We haven't planned anything yet."

"General, I understand. Of course, we would appreciate your keeping us apprised of any developments on your end. We will share details of any apparent HPM attack with your team."

"Sir Michael, I'll forward a WHITEHEAD top secret report summarizing what we've discovered so far."

"That would be splendid, old boy. I shall be watching for it. Can I share it with our two other WHITEHEAD team members?"

"Of course, Sir Michael. As long as they are still read into WHITEHEAD."

General Black hoped the signal intelligence lab could get the telemetry software loaded and tested in a few days—or less. He called Callahan to check their progress.

"Where are we with the satellite control system?"

Callahan was confident. "Sir, Robbie Chan has performed initial testing with the Cosmos 2455 satellite control signals in the lab and they're functioning as expected. We can have that software loaded by tomorrow on the Gulfstream and should be ready for use by COB. The aircraft must climb to flight level 420 over the Atlantic and fly under the satellite for at least three minutes of the pass. The orbit control effect should be immediate but may only shift the orbit by 5 degrees—the maximum during any one pass. If the satellite experiences multiple orbital shift control signals, it will use up its onboard fuel for orbit changes, which would end its usefulness."

"Great news, Callahan! Tell Chan that I will personally thank him and put him in for a special recognition award if the satellite control signals work. If he figures out how to deorbit Cosmos 2455, that would get him into the WEBMAZE SIGINT Hall of Fame."

The WEBMAZE Hall of Fame started with the first USSR satellite WEBMAZE successfully controlled. It was a classified list of just thirty-two names; like the stars on the wall at the CIA honoring their fallen, WEBMAZE critical players were listed on a wall plaque inside the WEBMAZE top secret secure area. Composed mostly of USAF military and civilians, there were also corporate names from RTW, ITQ, E-Logic, L2Cnet, MTREC, and Aerocorp.

Sergeant Alexander coordinated with the local police, who then decided to hire the Detective and Investigator Group to assist them in finding the truck. At 2200, detectives from the D&I Group driving their car along

Abay went into the nearest loading dock area. They didn't originally notice the truck. But when they went around to the other side, there it was, *Thomi's Pastry* plastered on the side.

"Headquarters, this is Detective Andreovich of the D&I Group. We have found the Thomi's Pastry truck. It is parked next to a building at the loading dock off Abay."

The two detectives parked, drew their pistols, and checked the cab first and then the rear. As they pried open the rear door, they found Nurlan, half asleep, sitting in his own piss and shit. "Finally! Get me out of here. The Americans kidnapped me and took my truck."

"Do you know where they went?"

"They said something about the Green Hotel on Abay."

The lead detective called Sergeant Alexander. "We have found the pastry truck abandoned in a harbor parking area. The driver was still in the back. He thinks the Americans said they would be meeting at the Green Hotel on Abay."

"Head over to the hotel and see if anyone saw them. If they have a video camera, check that too. Call me immediately if you find something."

Sergeant Alexander immediately called Evgeny, the Spetsnaz lead.

"Sergeant, we appreciate the update. Stake out the area and consider the possibility there might be a safe house nearby."

Evgeny called Director Arkonov, who was ecstatic.

"Great work! Contact the helo pilots, Anatoly and Boris, and have them monitor the docks for any unusual activity, starting at daybreak tomorrow."

34

THE TEAM ASSEMBLED after they got some rest and food under their belts. It was just after six and Rick and Jared were collecting the weapons. Brian and Susan got their mission equipment cases, and Walker discussed details of the exfil with Andrei.

"Brian, are you excited we're finally getting out of this place?" Susan asked.

"Yes, but I won't celebrate until we're in international waters. We're close but not there yet."

"I know the satphone is water resistant but not 'waterproof,' so keep it dry," Walker said.

All of their smartphones were already waterproof, so no problem there. Andrei's team had a weapons expert and a comm expert, both of whom were all business, getting ready.

"Colonel Walker, just in case we are discovered, my orders are to get you and your team to the Caspian Sea at all cost. If the FSB has figured out that your team is in Atyrau, they will have all possible escape routes covered—especially the sea route."

Walker agreed. "I understand your orders and that you won't surrender, but we also can't get captured. We'll attempt to fight our way to the Caspian right alongside your team. Do you have any heavy weapons like RPGs or machine guns onboard?"

Andrei was not surprised at the query since weapons were not discussed at the exfil meeting the night before.

"We'll be boarding a small but heavily armed and armored twelve-meter trawler. You will be pleasantly surprised with what the CIA gave us money to do. We will be bringing fishing gear to make it appear like a fishing expedition."

Walker was impressed. The CIA thought of everything, but if they were spotted, they'd still be outgunned. He hoped General Black had arranged for some muscle in case things went south.

Walker called it. "It's time—let's go."

The team followed Andrei to an electronically locked door in the back of the safe house structure. Andrei tapped in the code and opened what seemed like a 500-pound door to a tunnel just tall enough to walk through hunched over. It had minimal lighting and the floor was more cave-like than a typical walkway. It smelled of mold and the air was damp.

They approached another odd-looking door with a curious ship-like bulkhead wheel that Andrei turned to open. "On the other side of this door, there is a simple motor-driven pulley elevator that can hold four people at a time. I will go first with one of my men and two of yours," Andrei explained. "It goes up to a small storage building that we own and use for fishing tours."

"Mac, you come with me. The rest of you come up with Stanislav."

Minutes later, they were all assembled in the storage building waiting for Andrei's next move. "Follow me," he said, leading them to a bus with *Andrei's Fishing Tours* in both English and Russian on the side. "Everyone, grab a fishing pole from the rack over there and bring it with you when you board the bus. When we get to the trawler, make sure to take yours with you."

They each grabbed a pole and then boarded the bus. Andrei drove the bus out of the storage building and headed to the river port where the trawler was docked. Andrei yelled, "Do not get too comfortable; the drive is only fifteen minutes."

When the bus arrived at the dock, Andrei was a little concerned.

"There is a police car parked at each end of the parking lot. I will get out and walk to the boat with my pole and gear, then check out the boat. If nothing suspicious, I will honk the boat horn twice—one short and one long. When you hear the horn, get your gear and pole and walk casually to the boat."

Andrei jumped out with his fishing gear and walked to his trawler, named *Demon*. He didn't pay much attention to the police so as not to raise suspicion.

The boat was huge and there was a lot of prep work getting it started. Andrei went belowdecks and checked out every inch of space, especially the weapons cabinet and storage container. He concluded there was no threat on board, went to the captain's deck, honked the horn—one short and one long— and then turned on all the comm gear.

The tour bus occupants grabbed their poles and any other gear they needed and left the bus. Susan was getting cold feet and felt sick to her stomach as she picked up her suitcased equipment. She was the last one off. Brian waited for her, as Walker had requested, in case she got panicky. Andrei watched the police cars with his binoculars to see if they were watching the bus unload. Fortunately, they were preoccupied with their cell phones and missed the parade of fishermen to the boat. As they boarded, a helicopter came toward them from up the river in a low pass.

They were all on board when Andrei yelled, "Colonel Walker, get belowdecks with your team! A surveillance helicopter is coming overhead in a few seconds. Hurry!"

Seconds before the helicopter passed over them, the whole team got belowdecks and out of sight. Nobody saw them—or so they thought. A man was fishing off the dock about 150 feet away as the team boarded. He had seen the trawler *Demon* many times leaving the docks and traveling south along the Ural River. He knew it was a private charter fishing boat and thought, *I wish I could afford to go fishing on a large boat headed for the Caspian. I wonder how much it costs?*

That morning, police asked the Green Hotel manager if he had seen any of the people in the pictures he showed him. He said, "Nyet." The video camera was useless; it had broken months ago and no one had fixed it. The police asked some people out front if they had seen the Americans, showing their pictures.

One woman said, "I remember seeing them with boxes of pastries headed across Abay. They looked as though they were delivering them to a meeting. That is all I can remember."

The police split up and searched the whole neighborhood. When they went to the Taksim Café, Andrei's second-in-command denied ever seeing them. They were hitting a dead end.

After a few minutes of waiting and watching, Andrei started the engines and asked his men to cast off the lines and then make sure everything was working belowdecks.

The remote-control deck was first, food check was next, and last was weapons and ammo. The trawler had two RPGs, one Kalashnikov PKM, six AK-74s, ten Makarovs, and a small, compact rocket launcher. The PKM and rocket launcher were belowdecks but could be raised to topside with the pull of a lever. There was enough ammo to last a few hours in a firefight. With only Andrei and two crew members, they were still outmanned.

Andrei said, "Stanislav, show Rick and Jared where all the weapons and ammo are. Show them how to set up the PKM and rocket launcher."

Jared was impressed. "This tug boat's like an armory. It's got more weapons and ammo than some outposts I've been assigned to!"

"Don't get too excited," Rick warned. "We're like sitting ducks if they find us. Recall the riverboats in Vietnam got beat up pretty badly in firefights."

35

THE BAIKONUR COSMODROME aerospace engineers were elated that their overhead asset was working flawlessly. They declared it partially operational and decided that after the next operational test success, they would declare full operational capability. They were controlling the orbital shift to test HPM penetration into below-ground structures, which was why they chose the London Underground.

Richard Callahan had good news for General Black.

"Sir, the L2Cnet Gulfstream is ready to go. The software has been loaded and tested as well."

"Is there a mission operator available and are you ready to execute the mission?"

"Yes sir. The L2Cnet flight and mission crews are ready and waiting your order. They know the Cosmos 2455 orbital parameters and can fly beneath it for the required telemetry command signal period."

"Best news yet, Callahan! I'll contact the L2Cnet team directly and give them the official order. You and your team did a great job in a very short time. Let's get this show on the road!"

General Black called General Erik Holloway, USAF chief of staff, and discussed the situation. "Erik, the DEPRESSION bird is ready to launch. We need POTUS to approve the satellite control action. Have you had that discussion?"

"Joe, President Marr understands the timeliness of the situation. With approvals from Sheffield and Denzer, he approved an immediate launch. He expects immediate reporting on what happens. His only concern was that if the Russians found out what was happening, they might mount a counteraction of some kind. I'll inform NSA director Duffy to listen for any counteraction comms."

"Thanks. I'll keep you informed as to progress," said an elated General Black.

After a brief STE conversation with the L2Cnet program manager and a lieutenant colonel in charge of DEPRESSION activities, the L2Cnet Gulfstream took off and flew parallel to the orbit over the east coast. The telemetry orbital maneuver control signal was sent and then they waited. The next pass was much farther east, so they would need to land at Pease AFB to refuel for the next Atlantic pass. Again, they flew under the orbit sending the orbit maneuver command signal.

The Russian cosmodrome engineers watched the satellite shift orbit too far east. They tried readjusting the orbit during the pass over Baikonur, but it was already too far east in a new orbit. They panicked, thinking that the software might be corrupted, and decided to send a reboot command. The reboot took almost fifteen minutes. By the time the satellite came back into view, it was so far off the planned test orbit that they had to cancel the London test.

Callahan called General Black. "Good news. The satellite orbital maneuver control telemetry appears to be working as expected. The orbit is no longer going over London, so we are waiting to see what the Russians do next."

"Excellent, Callahan! The Russians are probably confused and attempting to correct the orbit. How many orbital maneuvers can the satellite perform before it runs out of maneuver fuel and loses the ability to change orbits?"

"Sir, I suspect that due to the much larger mass of the HPM system, the Russians may have planned for hundreds of major orbital maneuvers."

"So, does that mean it will take hundreds of flights to exhaust all their maneuver fuel?"

"Actually, no sir. The excessive orbital repositioning maneuvers will likely force them to use up more than the nominal fuel for a typical orbital maneuver due to the incidental effects drag and gravity will have on their satellite."

"In English, Callahan."

"Sir, think of it this way; an aircraft that flies a course into a headwind uses more fuel than flying with a tailwind. We're creating the equivalent of a headwind."

"That still doesn't answer the question. How much longer will we need to override the Russian orbital maneuvering?"

"Sir, that would depend on the initial amount of orbital maneuver thruster fuel on board, which we don't know. We've initiated a perturbation that might result in a divergent instability, but we won't know that for some time."

The cosmodrome engineers were perplexed. Every pass they attempted to shift the orbit west, it seemed to go farther east. It was as though the software had a bug—or a mind of its own. But why had it worked correctly for all the prior tests and not now?

"There must be a hardware failure that we are not seeing," said one engineer.

Meanwhile, the Cosmos 2455 orbits kept shifting east—regardless of the cosmodrome orbital control signals sent. In an effort to regain control, the Pacific and Atlantic remote operations satellite control ships were activated and commanded to send westerly orbital control shift signals to the satellite as well. Nothing seemed to work.

As the trawler *Demon* wound its way south along the Ural, Andrei noticed police parked sporadically along the banks. He did not know that the FSB had set up an intercept point just before the Ural emptied into the Caspian. Inbound boats were allowed to pass without incident, but every outbound boat and ship were being boarded and inspected by a Spetsnaz team. The trawler was just forty-five minutes from the choke point when Walker's satphone lit up.

"This is Ops Center. Colonel Walker, we're monitoring the situation where the Ural feeds into the Caspian with an RQ-4 Hawk; there's an armed choke point boarding all outgoing vessels. In addition to the Global Hawk, there's a fully armed Reaper on its way—ETA fifty mikes. Do NOT slow down at the boarding request. Speed up; defend the ship as best you can and get into international waters as fast as possible."

"Ops Center—message acknowledged. Are you prepared for an extraction?"

"Sir, the rendezvous vessel is over an hour away heading to your position. At this time, you need to get into international waters any way possible."

"Understood. The trawler has light defensive weapons only, but we'll make good use of 'em. Thanks for the intel; we owe you one!"

"Good luck. Ops Center out."

Walker immediately turned to Andrei's crew and yelled, "Just got intel that there's likely a Spetsnaz team boarding all outgoing vessels. Ops Center is monitoring the situation. We should be there in about forty-five minutes. They recommend ignoring all boarding requests and speeding to international waters while defending the ship. How fast can this tug go?"

"No problem, Colonel Walker," Andrei said. "This ship can do more than forty knots, and at that rate, we will be in international waters in about fifteen minutes."

"What kind of trawler does forty knots?" asked Rick.

"This trawler is special. It was, as you Americans say, 'tricked out' with high-powered motors, hydrofoils, and a rocket-resistant hull. Everyone must go belowdecks when we ramp up speed. We can defend the ship from sea and air attacks but not until we are up on the hydrofoils."

Walker was impressed. "Let me guess—the CIA?"

Andrei laughed, "Of course, the CIA was very generous with the Taksim Café and this trawler. Very cool, da?"

"I'll personally thank the CIA folks for footing the bill to 'trick out' this boat," Walker said.

"Have you ever gotten her to max speed?" Rick asked.

"Of course. We were doing sea trials in the Caspian just four months ago. Yuri, take over the helm. I want to bring Colonel Walker belowdecks to show him the weapon systems, remote operations area, and engine room. The weapons are fairly easy to operate. Your sergeants learned quickly."

The cosmodrome satellite control engineers rebooted the onboard computers one at a time, hoping to clear any memory glitches. To their shock, the orbit changed again—without a command. They were losing control of Cosmos 2455 and so decided to engage the failsafe mode, which turned off the encryption. After two passes, the orbit appeared to stabilize, so it was decided to turn the encryption back on. The orbits shifted again; they suspected the encryption algorithm was corrupted. The satellite had drifted so far out of its planned orbit it would take two weeks of orbit corrections to get back.

Before they could send a signal to Cosmos 2455 to reset the encryption algorithm, the satellite appeared to deorbit on its own. The cosmodrome engineers panicked and activated the orbital thrusters to push it back into its normal orbit, but instead Cosmos 2455 continued to deorbit—without explanation. For two passes, the satellite orbit was not affected by their control signals, so they suspected that the thrusters were spent or not functioning. Then a telemetry status message indicated low fuel for the orbit maneuver thrusters.

The WEBMAZE team got excellent feedback reports from the onboard operators of the Gulfstream telemetry system. As they monitored the orbital changes, they hoped the thrusters would eventually run out of fuel. They were all surprised when the satellite dropped lower in orbit than on the previous pass. Cosmos 2455 appeared to be in an unpredictable death spiral.

36

THE RIDE ALONG the winding Ural river was scenic and peaceful. Walker thought, *The calm before the storm.* All the while, Andrei pointed out interesting sights along the Ural River banks. Birds were especially plentiful, and many were large and crane-like. Rick couldn't hold back.

"You'll be a great sightseeing tour guide for your next career."

"The Ural gets really shallow in some spots and unless you are very careful, it is easy to hit bottom and get stuck," Andrei said. "The delta forms what is known as a digitate where many branches of the river form smaller deltas due to the silt buildup. That is where the best fishing is."

The two fast attack boats the intel described appeared about 400 yards ahead of the *Demon*. Andrei yelled, "We've got company!"

As the trawler approached the closest of the two fast attack boats, Andrei saw someone waving. A few seconds later, a stern-sounding voice blared over a marine radio speaker in Russian, "Slow down and stop your trawler! Be prepared to be boarded. If you refuse our orders, we will shoot to kill."

Andrei sped up a bit and signaled back, honking the horn in acknowledgment. Andrei yelled, "Everyone belowdecks! We are about to be fired on!" The hand waving got more animated as Andrei waved back and ignored the command. The radio blared again.

"This is your final warning; stop or we will fire!" Then there was a short machine-gun burst across the bow, a nonlethal warning of last resort. Andrei gunned the engines and ducked below the six-inch-thick conning tower wall. Bullets sprayed the side of the conning tower and the hull, bouncing off with a twang. Andrei operated the ship from a remote-control box with a display of the view ahead from one of two video cameras in the bow and one of two in the stern—another feature paid for by the CIA.

Bullets hit everywhere but to no avail. The trawler bounced around due to the waves at the mouth of the Caspian, but it plowed through them faster and faster. In less than fifteen seconds the trawler was at full speed, but the fast attack boats easily kept up with it.

"Stanislav and Yuri—engage weapons now!" Up popped a PKM from belowdecks, sporting an integrated bullet shield, with Yuri at the trigger. The mini rocket launcher popped up next with Stanislav at the controls. Rick assisted reloads of the PKM for Yuri, and Jared reloaded the rocket launcher for Stanislav. The rocket launcher hit its mark on the third try, destroying the closest attack boat.

Andrei saw an attack helicopter closing in behind them on his rearview video and told Yuri, "Get rid of the helo." Andrei didn't see the second helicopter higher up in front of the trawler flying backwards until it was firing onto the deck. Yuri was hit in the right shoulder, so Rick took over the PKM.

Pouring lead into the rear helicopter, Rick took it out with a hail of bullets. It started to gyro and eventually dove into the water, spinning as it entered. Rick fired at the second fast boat. Bullets from the forward attack helicopter strafed the deck, homing in on the mini rocket launcher. Stanislav rotated the mini rocket launcher to fire on the helicopter, fired and missed twice.

Jared yelled to Stanislav, "We only have three more rockets!"

Andrei now saw that the delta was way behind the *Demon*. He yelled, "We are now in international waters. Keep defending the ship!" Just then, the helicopter firing onto the bow blew up in a big fireball, its debris raining on the trawler. A few seconds later, the fast boat that moments earlier was zigzagging and closing in disappeared in another ball of flames. Walker looked up from belowdecks and yelled, "A Reaper?"

The trawler hummed along at forty-two knots with no one following. Susan patched up Yuri's bullet wound in the shoulder with Brian assisting. Brian still had an AK-74 strapped to his back in case the trawler got boarded. Walker came up from belowdecks with his Glock ready to back up Andrei if he were injured.

"I guess your DoD comrades really want you back!" Andrei joked.

"Yeah, too much investment by the DoD to fail! Besides, SOCOM practices for this shit. We're probably the first to actually live it!" said Walker.

Rick and Jared came up to the main deck. Rick asked, "Did a Reaper just take out the helo and the pursuit boat?"

"Yup. Silent but deadly," Walker said. "Request for support? Check!" Walker came up to the trawler's control tower. "Andrei, I doubt the Russians will give up just because we're in international waters. We should expect another attack before we get to the rescue ship."

"That is a strong possibility, but Russia has limited resources for additional attack helicopters, so we should be free and clear," Andrei said.

Walker's satphone buzzed.

"Colonel Walker, kudos on defense of the trawler! Watched and recorded it all with the Hawk. Hope the Hellfires didn't do any collateral damage to the trawler! ETA of rescue ship is twenty mikes. The Reaper will loiter a little longer."

"Thanks, and good shooting! Acknowledge rendezvous with rescue ship in twenty mikes."

"You're welcome, Colonel. Ops Center out."

Walker was thankful that the general had the MQ-9 tasked. He knew the ground control station, or GCS, for the Hawks were at Beale but wondered where the GCS for the Reaper was from. *Schriever? Creech? Local?*

Andrei called his recovery team on his satphone. "Get the bus off the dock and back in the warehouse. We have to change the identity of the trawler, so we won't be back for at least two weeks."

Walker called General Black.

"Nice work getting your team out of Kazakhstan! Is everyone okay? I heard that you had to defend the trawler from both an air and sea attack."

"Sir, I'll admit, it was dicey for a few minutes before the Reaper showed up. My team is okay, but one of Andrei's guys took a hit. So, what's happening with 2455?"

"Steve, I can't tell you everything now, but your team was the critical link in the chain."

"Sir, we all knew it had to get done. This mission was way more intense than prior missions."

"Your team overcame some really tough obstacles because of the insider threat. Call me from the rescue ship. I can explain more about the satellite at that time."

"Sir, you should know that the Russian safe house team from the Taksim Café really came through. The CIA's investment was worth every penny! Agent out."

Just as Walker headed to his team to report the pickup by a Ukrainian-flagged trawler minutes away, two rockets hit the trawler, taking out the mini rocket launcher. Fortunately, Stanislav and Jared weren't there.

Andrei, looking around for the threat, heard a distinctive muffled turbine engine and yelled, "UCAV attack! Stanislav, get to the PKM—shoot it down. Everyone else—belowdecks!"

Walker, Susan, and Brian jumped down to the lower deck and went into the trawler's hull. Even as Andrei zigzagged the boat, another anti-ship Kh-31A rocket from a lone Mikoyan Skat UCAV hit the rear of the trawler, blowing a hole in the stern and almost taking out the propulsion system. Jared got to the PKM before Stanislav, dragged it over to where the mini rocket launcher used to be, and set up. Stanislav followed Jared with the ammo cans, prepared to feed the weapon. Another rocket flashed, with Andrei watching this time, allowing him to maneuver out of the rocket's trajectory. Everyone fell to the deck. The little UCAV was hard to see, but when Jared saw the flash he started firing at it. Soon a streak of smoke billowed behind the drone, which looked like a miniature B-2 bomber in all white. It climbed, Jared pumping more lead into its ventral surface. It did a wing-over, and in a few seconds flames were shooting out from the rear. It flew into a stall configuration, and then, in a desperate attempt to stabilize, it nosed over, rolled to the left, and fired another Kh31A straight into the water.

The UCAV followed, diving into the Caspian. The rocket hit the water just fifty yards behind the *Demon* and blew up. It shook the trawler as Andrei pushed the throttle.

"That was close," Andrei said. "That's a nasty and lethal little drone. Fortunately for us, better designed for going after ground targets."

Walker, amazed that the *Demon* survived the attack, said, "Wow—a UCAV against us? And clearly in international waters!"

"Your team must have really pissed off the FSB!" Andrei said. "That UCAV was worth a quarter billion rubles!"

Jared, enjoying a moment of victory, said, "A few hundred bucks of bullets just neutralized a quarter-billion-ruble UCAV! Never underestimate the effectiveness of a well-placed round!"

Susan and Brian were still below deck tending to Yuri's shoulder wound. Susan asked Brian, "Do you think we're safe now?"

"With this team, I would never doubt that for a second."

Andrei, Walker, Jared, and Stanislav were waiting for the third wave when an SH60 Seahawk approached the boat. Using the external loudspeaker, the Seahawk pilot announced, "Russian trawler *Demon*, this is Seahawk Xray Foxtrot 18 here to support the rendezvous. If you have a radio, key it three times—five seconds each time."

Long-range reconnaissance Seahawks had a multi-spectrum software-tunable radio system that covered 30 to 400 MHz and could lock onto a radio transmission frequency and modulation within two transmissions. Andrei had a standard maritime VHF radio and a multiband military ARC-210 onboard, so he chose the ARC-210 in UHF AM mode at 325 MHz—unencrypted. He pressed the push-to-talk key three times, five seconds each time.

"Trawler *Demon*, we have you on 325 MHz in AM. Please acknowledge."

"Seahawk Xray Foxtrot 18, this is Andrei Zharkov, captain of the fishing trawler *Demon* with special passengers for rendezvous—over."

"Captain Zharkov, please put Colonel Steve Walker on. Over."

"Seahawk Xray Foxtrot 18, this is Lieutenant Colonel Steve Walker—special ops team leader. Over."

"Colonel Walker—this is Lieutenant Robert Powers, team leader of SBT-20. We were contacted by General Black's XO to escort you to the rescue ship, ten mikes out. If you need immediate assistance, we can either drop down or pick up, over."

Walker looked at Andrei and said, "Is Yuri okay, or would you like him to get immediate attention?"

Andrei looked at Yuri, laughed, and then said, "I think he can wait the ten minutes!"

Walker pressed the PTT button. "Lieutenant Powers, okay for now. The escort is appreciated. Watch for UCAVs; we were just attacked by one a few minutes ago. Over."

"Roger that, sir. Monitored that scenario unfolding via a Hawk rebroadcast. Flying escort to your rendezvous. See you in a few mikes. Over."

As the SH-60 hovered directly overhead, Susan realized the threat of capture was finally lifting. "Wow, that was far more adventure than I signed up for. No offense, guys, but I think I'll be moving on to safer tasks in support of DoD."

"No offense taken," Brian said. "We signed up for this kind of crap, but civilians don't. You should know, we couldn't have done this without you!"

Rick and Jared both yelled, "Ditto."

"Maybe, but I need to take a bath, eat real food, get a manicure and some peace and quiet!"

Walker was more grateful. "Mac, you should know we would have protected you with our lives. Your home-base team will soon understand how critical you were to the success of this mission."

Walker then turned to Andrei, "You guys really came through—high speed trawler, heavy machine guns, and a mini rocket launcher—I'm impressed. You saved our butts."

Andrei looked at his two-man team and said, "None of us are fans of Putin or his regime. But we could not have done this without a huge investment by the CIA. I never thought we would actually employ all of *Demon*'s capabilities. We will find a safe haven to rename the *Demon*, change its appearance, and get it back in good shape again."

"I'll bet my boss is working that aspect of things as we speak," Walker said. "He's influential with this sort of coverage. I won't be surprised if your next contact is a CIA operative."

37

FSB DIRECTOR ARKONOV reluctantly answered the phone on his desk.

"Yes, General Alekseyev . . ."

"Apparently you just cost the Russian government billions of rubles in military hardware, the loss of highly skilled Spetsnaz, and stolen satellite technology. Your ineptness allowed the American spies to escape Kazakhstan along with critical satellite intelligence!"

"Sir, I can explain why—"

"Director Arkonov, I do not care why you failed. That is for an FSB tribunal to decide. You are relieved of duty as of now; your deputy will assume responsibility for all FSB counterintelligence operations. You are to report to the headquarters in Moscow tomorrow morning—no later than eleven."

The engineers and scientists at the Baikonur Cosmodrome were helpless as their prized satellite, Cosmos 2455, deorbited at an accelerated pace. They had tried everything. There was nothing that they could do except track it. It was entering the upper atmosphere over the south Pacific and they predicted the reentry point would be over the Azores—not too far north of Pico Island. They notified the vehicle recovery team, and within minutes they mobilized and started flying to the north Atlantic. The possibility of recovering the satellite was slim to none since it was not designed for reentry. It would most likely burn up during entry into the upper atmosphere.

General Black got the news from WEBMAZE team leader Callahan.

"Sir, Cosmos 2455 is deorbiting instead of orbit shifting, and it's happening at a faster pace than predicted. We think the continuous orbital change command telemetry signals eventually destabilized the satellite, forcing it to roll on its side, and then pushed its orbit downward instead of sideways. It is doomed to start reentry in the south Pacific region and will most likely burn up in the north Atlantic—probably over the Azores. Will you need to send a satellite recovery team to recover any debris?"

"Callahan, that's the best news I've heard in five years! Track its descent into the Atlantic and let me know when it hits. And, no, I don't see the point in fighting the Russians over a scrap of burned-up satellite hardware!"

"Sir, the WEBMAZE team would like to know more about the satellite's configuration and structure! We would also like to confirm the HPM design! Cosmos 2455 has huge 'capture' value."

"Sorry, Callahan, we don't have the resources in place and, in any case, you can bet the Russians are already on their way to the Azores. You WEBMAZE techs really came through for us! You're all great patriots!"

After boarding the Ukrainian rescue ship, Walker's satphone rang. "Sir, we are all safe and sound—my team, Andrei's team, and the rescue team. Why didn't you tell me about the Reapers? I didn't expect them."

"Congrats, Steve, on a job well done. It's a plus when everyone RTBs in one piece. Thanks to your field team, we not only got control of 2455, but deorbited it as well! It'll be hitting the Atlantic north of the Azores. The Reaper was in nearby Ukraine but had to be flown over the Black Sea, refueled in Georgia, and flown through Azerbaijan airspace in order to evade the Russians. Heard that it was helpful, eh, Colonel?"

"Sir, are you saying our intercept data was already used in a mission against 2455? Seriously? It's barely three days since our last intercept mission."

"I had to put a little pressure on Callahan, but he and his team pulled it off."

Walker pondered the huge satellite entering the atmosphere. "That thing's gonna leave a big mess in its wake because of its size and mass."

General Black agreed. "We expect it to be a huge fireball upon reentry. We still don't think the Russians know what happened! The fate of 2455 was a team effort, and your team was on the pointy end of that spear. In case you're wondering, Vladimir is safe and sound at his horse ranch. We made sure he had an alibi and a clean restart. Unfortunately, we lost the two safe houses. When you get back—and you are settled in at the vault—write up the field report. Expect a debriefing in a few days. We need to learn what worked well and what didn't. Make sure the TOP SECRET SI/TK report includes US/UK/CAN/AUS ONLY under the WEBMAZE code word. See you when you get back! Safe travels, out."

At 1447 local time, Azores, Cosmos 2455 reentered the atmosphere in the form of a few large and hundreds of smaller fireballs. The people on Pico Island thought it was a meteor shower. The Russians searched a debris field over 400 miles long and a mile wide for weeks and found nothing larger than an antenna connector.

Two more names were added to the WEBMAZE Hall of Fame: Susan "Mac" MacDonald and Robbie Chan, just as General Black promised.

Just three weeks after the Cosmos 2455 mission debrief, Lieutenant Colonel Walker and his AQUADUCT field team, including Mac, were called into General Black's WEBMAZE office. The general got right to the point.

"There's a situation in the South China Sea that requires the skills of a special signal intercept team . . ."

AUTHOR'S NOTE

Although the people and events portrayed in this novel are fiction, the brave and determined men and women of the US Department of Defense work tirelessly to defend the country against every threat—ground, sea, air, cyber, and space—day or night, 24/7. All recent secretaries of defense have agreed: Space is rapidly becoming the next contested battle-zone, and eventually, even with signed treaties, there will be a need to defend satellites in all orbits: LEO, MEO, and GEO. Working with our allies, space threats can be identified and managed, and, as a last resort, neutralized.

ACKNOWLEDGMENTS

This book would not have been possible if it weren't for the assistance and guidance of the following: Dan Sanchez, LtC USAF (Retired), who proofread the initial manuscript for errors; Judith Coughlin-Sanchez, who provided guidance on enhancing the storyline, dialogue, and character presentation; and Laurie, my wife of over forty-nine years, for critical suggestions on improving the sensibility and readability of the scenarios and for tips when I had writer's block. I must also thank Joe Coccaro and Hannah Woodlan, the editors at Koehler. Some of the material in this novel was derived from work performed as an engineer in the areas of military intelligence, surveillance, and reconnaissance (ISR), and through program affiliations with defense contractors through my career. Lastly, my experience in the Army Security Agency while serving with the 175th Radio Research Group in Bien Hoa, Vietnam also helped to develop some of the scenarios.

Credits

CPSIA information can be obtained
at www.ICGtesting.com
Printed in the USA
LVHW110207300120
645289LV00001B/26